Diary of an ACCIDENTAL WITCH

WITCH

FLYING HIGH

PERDITA & HONOR CARGILL
ILLUSTRATED BY KATIE SAUNDERS

LITTLE TIGER
LONDON

VERY, VERY PRIVATE TOP SECRET

PROPERTY OF BEA BLACK

1 Piggoty Lane,
Little Spellshire,
Spellshire

WARNING: Serious risk of being turned into a toad if you read this diary…

CH:

Great fun!"
iPaper

"...full of comedy with moving moments
of heartwarming magic. Totally spellbinding!"
Lancashire Evening Post

"Full of magical mayhem!"
BookTrust

"A magical adventure that will touch your heart
and tickle your funny bone. I loved it."
Maz Evans, author of WHO LET THE GODS OUT

"The new Worst Witch! Full of charm and chuckles.
Kids are going to LOVE it."
Abi Elphinstone, author of JUNGLEDROP

"A brilliant, hilarious story!"
Emma Carroll, author of LETTERS FROM THE LIGHTHOUSE

"Love, love, loved it! It made me smile
the whole way through!"
Jennifer Killick author of CRATER LAKE

"Super sparky, funny and brimming
with magic and imagination."
Andy Shepherd, author of THE BOY WHO GREW DRAGONS

TO ELLA WHID[...]
OUR MAGICAL [...]

FOR ARCHIE A[...]

STRIPES PUBLISHING LIMITED
An imprint of the Little Tiger Group
1 Coda Studios, 189 Munster Road, London SW6 6AW

Imported into the EEA by Penguin Random House Ireland,
Morrison Chambers, 32 Nassau Street, Dublin D02 YH68

A paperback original
First published in Great Britain in 2022

MIX
Paper from
responsible sources
FSC® C171272

The Forest Stewardship Council® (FSC®) is a global, not-for-profit
organization dedicated to the promotion of responsible forest management
worldwide. FSC defines standards based on agreed principles for responsible
forest stewardship that are supported by environmental, social, and
economic stakeholders. To learn more, visit www.fsc.org

10 9 8 7 6 5 4 3 2 1

MONDAY 1ST NOVEMBER

11:03am Home

It's the first day of half-term, I'm still in my pyjamas and I've had three biscuits for breakfast and half a packet of fluffmallows that I found under my pillow. What is even more impressive is that I managed to *levitate* the fluffmallows with my WAND all the way from the bed to my mouth.

It feels weird writing in a new diary. The pages are so empty and there are almost no crossings-outs or mistakes or missed days or lists of things I have NOT managed to do (like potion spells). It's so clean and perf—

1

11:11am

The thing about fluffmallows is that they are very STICKY.

I've hidden the old diary at the back of my sock drawer because it is *very* important that NO ONE ever reads it. Especially not Dad because I never did learn to write in code  —EDOC? FRGH? £0D*? — and it will only take him about a nanosecond to find out that I'm a ~~witch~~ witch-in-training. That's the sort of shock nobody wants to give a parent.

I feel bad keeping such a big secret from Dad, but it's his own fault for making us move to Little Spellshire and *then* accidentally sending me to the School of Extraordinary Arts instead of the perfectly ordinary **Spellshire Academy**. If it hadn't been for that one tiny classic-Dad-muddle-up, I probably still wouldn't even know witches *existed*, far less be learning how to become one.

Witches, when they're not hanging out with other

witches (like at WITCH SCHOOL), are very hush-hush about their witchiness. As our headmistress, Ms Sparks, always says, 'Those of us who know, *know* and those of them who don't, *can't.*'

So, even though Dad's mistake turned out to be the most brilliant mistake in the history of mistakes, I can't tell him. If I did, I'd probably have to turn him into a toad* or maybe Ms Sparks would turn *me* into a toad – or maybe we'd BOTH be turned into toads. (I can't really imagine any of my teachers turning somebody into a toad, but I've learned the hard way that in Little Spellshire it's best not to rule anything out.)

11:22am

I *can* imagine some people in my class turning ME into a toad.

Hunter Gunn? Izzi Geronimo?

Definitely Blair Smith-Smythe!

*NO IDEA how to do this.

12:04pm

"Bea!" Ash is leaning out of his bedroom window and yelling across the gap between our houses. "Half-term!"

We grin at each other. We might go to *very* different schools – no witchiness for anyone at the **Academy** – but we both have a whole week of no lessons ahead.

"Put that diary down and come over. Mum's baking."

I'm very tempted because Mrs Namdar's cakes are the best *non*-witchy cakes in the universe and I can already smell cinnamon wafting out of their kitchen window, but I've got less than twenty minutes to get out of my pyjamas and over to Taffy Tallywick's Teashop to meet Winnie and Puck and Fabi and Amara.

"I can't!" I shout back. "I'm meeting friends from school."

Ash looks a bit disappointed and I nearly ask him to come with me but a) there's the ~~huge~~ little problem of no one from his school talking to anyone who goes to my school and b) the ~~enormous~~ slightly bigger problem that if Ash found out about even ~~half a quarter~~ ONE PER CENT of what happens at Extraordinary then I'd have to start worrying about people being turned into toads again. There are a lot of secrets in Little Spellshire.

"Morning, you two!" Dad shouts up from the garden. "Come outside! It's such a glorious day."

It is super sunny and warm, which would be odd for November except that Little Spellshire is home to the weirdest weather in the world (which makes my weather-scientist dad very happy and is the reason we moved here).

"Twenty-three degrees Celsius with a light south-westerly breeze!" he shouts. "Not the sort of morning – or should I say *afternoon* – to waste indoors."

Aaaarrgh! I'm going to be late meeting my friends and I'm still not dressed.

2:31pm

Just got home from Taffy's.

"Why are you wearing pyjamas?" was the first thing Amara said when I walked into the teashop. I'd have pretended it was a style statement (how could neon-green pyjamas *not* be in style?) except that the last time they saw me – at the Halloween Ball – I was dressed as a frog so I didn't exactly have a track record as a fashion influencer. Anyway, it wasn't like the rest of them were dressed sensibly...

Winnie

Fabi

Amara

Puck

"I wish it could be **Halloween** again," I said, watching Taffy take down yesterday's decorations. I'd never known how much fun **Halloween** could be until I'd come to Little Spellshire and made friends with witches.

"Never mind **Halloween**," said Winnie, "it's only *fifty* days until—"

"**Winter Solstice!**" chorused Fabi, Puck and Amara.

"Er ... what's **Winter Solstice**?" I asked.

"It's the longest and witchiest night of the year," Winnie explained patiently.

"There's a big *party*," added Puck with a grin.

I was beginning to realize that witches really liked parties – and that was good because now I had friends in Little Spellshire I liked parties again too.

"We all wear masks to represent the creatures in the *Great Ode to the Winter Solstice* and dance round a huge bonfire and feast on yummy things," said Amara, dividing up a slice of Taffy's famous chocolate fudge cake for us to share.

"But before that," announced Fabi, "there's the **Grand Tournament**!"

"The **Grand Tournament**?"

"It's only the biggest, SPORTIEST day in the witchy calendar!" Fabi grinned.

"You'll love it, Bea," said Puck. "Lots of **GO** matches."

GO! Something I liked even more than *bonfire parties*! My favourite witch sport* – and more fun than any non-witch sport.

"And inter-year broom speed races and chimney-scoring contests and flying displays and the No-Rules-Anything-Could-Happen-Teacher/Student-Contest," added Amara through a mouthful of crumbs.

Fifty days was too long to wait!

We were making plans to practise broom-racing before we went back to school (or 'refereeing' in Winnie's** case) when the door to the teashop swung open, blowing in a blast of hot air and three *extremely* tidy teenagers who definitely did not go to Extraordinary. It was a relief when they went to sit

*Possibly ONLY witch sport??
**Least sporty witch EVER.

at the furthest table because, although we could feel them staring at us, they probably couldn't hear what we were saying.

"Imagine *them* playing **GO**," said Puck and we all got the giggles so badly that Taffy had to come over and ask us to calm down.

But now I'm back home I'm feeling bad about laughing because, although there *is* something funny about the idea of non-witches (the 'Ordinaries' – that's what everyone at school calls them) flying about on broomsticks, I HATE it when people in this town talk about 'them' and 'us'.

HALF-TERM HOMEWORK

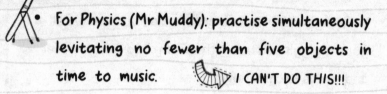

- For Physics (Mr Muddy): practise simultaneously levitating no fewer than five objects in time to music. I CAN'T DO THIS!!!

- For Chemistry (Miss Lupo): collect specimens of sneezewort and mad dogweed. (On this occasion, students are permitted to collect the specimens directly from the forest, but only during daylight and they must work in groups of at least three witches. DO NOT GO BEYOND TOADSTOOL HOLLOW.)

- For English (Madam Binx): write a rhyming incantation of no fewer than six lines. The incantation MUST include words that rhyme with 'piggle'.

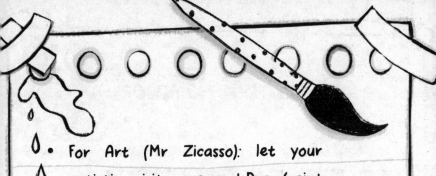

- For Art (Mr Zicasso): let your artistic spirit move you! Draw/paint whatever you want!

- For Zoology (Prof Agu): spend at least half an hour contemplating the earthworm and make a list of its magical properties.

- For History (Professor Crisp): talk to your grandparents or other important elderly people in your life about their favourite famous witches and make notes to share with the class.

- For Maths (Mr Smith): practise the eight times table so often that you can recite it backwards.

TUESDAY 2ND NOVEMBER

11:51am Home

It's not even lunchtime and I've ticked one thing off my homework list!

Worms are *amazing*. Especially the one I accidentally cut in half with my spade and which is now TWO worms. Zoology? Or *magic*?

7:12pm

It's taken me all day, but I've finished my art homework too! As worm portraits go, I think it's pretty good.

Worm

B. Black, Year Seven

5:55am Home

It's pitch-black and practically the middle of the night, but Winnie says dawn is the very best time to collect sneezewort.

I don't want to wake Dad so I'll leave him a note.

Going to the forest for homework. May be some time x

7:31pm Home (again, finally!)

Dad was going bananas by the time I got back. He's normally chill about me going off on my own (and VERY enthusiastic about anything to do with homework), but apparently my note had not been as *reassuring* as I'd hoped.

"WHAT HAPPENED TO YOU?!" he roared as I came through the door. "You look like you've been dragged through a hedge backwards."

Close. I'd actually *fallen into* a hedge backwards – well, several hedges, a patch of sticky willie and an especially spiky bramble bush. To be fair, the forest is very tangly and the sneezewort hadn't been easy to get to.

"AND WHY ARE YOU ALL WET?!"

Um, because I'd fallen off my broomstick into Cauldron Pond, but Dad probably didn't need to know that.

"There was a sudden and surprising shower of *very* heavy rain," I fibbed, and because it was Little Spellshire, and anything could happen when it came to the weather (or, come to think about it, just about anything else), he believed me.

"I was with my friends," I explained.

We'd had such a fun day – forest-exploring and accidental-pond-swimming and werewolf-ghost-storytelling and especially flying.

"Humph! All I knew was that you weren't with Ash because he came round looking for you ... *twice*. You've been gone all day!"

That was mostly because we'd had to go as far as Tangle Patch to find a clearing big enough for broom-racing and where the wych elms were tall enough for secrecy. Obviously, I couldn't tell Dad that so I produced some slightly squashed but very tasty blackberries as a bribe and eventually he calmed down.

7:45pm

As usual, Dad burned the fish fingers, but we feasted on squishy blackberries and custard creams for dinner. *Yum.*

9:10pm

Ghosty-werewolf stories aren't so much fun when you're alone. It's a pity Ash isn't awake (I shouted over, but his curtains were closed).

10:11pm

I'm sure I can hear *howling*.

Ash would have had so much fun with us today. I'll hang out with him tomorrow.

dogweed

THURSDAY 4TH NOVEMBER

10:55am Home

Puck and Fabi and Winnie have come to collect me.
It turns out we need to go back to the forest because
we forgot to collect any mad dogweed. It shouldn't
take long and I'll go and see Ash as soon as I get back.

8:33pm

Mad dogweed is really hard to find! I'll hang out with
Ash tomorrow.

FRIDAY 5TH NOVEMBER

10:00am Home

If this was term time, I'd be playing a **GO** match for real right now – Dodos (my team) against the Dragons (Blair's team). It's not that I *want* half-term to end, but I CANNOT WAIT to get back on the pitch again!

10:09am

I'm not the only one missing flying. Puck and Amara have just turned up to drag me off to the forest for **GO** practice.

4:55pm Tangle Patch, the forest

Time disappears when you're on a broom.

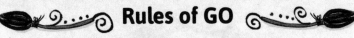

Rules of GO

(Based on the original rules drawn up by

Mistress Quick in 1567)

The **aim of the game** is to score more points than the opposing team. This is achieved by hitting or throwing the ball down the Great Chimney. Players are encouraged to deploy approved GO tactics (consult the Extraordinary GO tactic cards for more information). Points are deducted if the ball ends up in the wrong chimney and for fouls (see over page).

Each game lasts for forty-five minutes: two halves of twenty minutes with a five-minute break for players to calm down.

GOers must wear PE uniform with optional GO gloves and a sports bib in the team colours. Rainbow capes must be worn for the Winter Solstice Grand Tournament.

There are ten players a side: nine GOers, one Sweep. GOers may pass the ball from team member to team member only by a) throwing or b) using their broom in the style of a bat. GOers must attempt to stay mounted on the broom at all times.

The role of the Sweep is to record the score. When the ball is successfully thrown down the Great Chimney, it will temporarily take on the colour of the team that has made the strike; that colour is recorded by both Sweeps when the ball rolls out of the grate below. At the same moment as the ball disappears into the chimney, a new ball will magically appear at the centre of the pitch and will immediately be in play. When the Sweeps are not recording goals, they should at least attempt to keep fit by occasionally jumping up and down on the spot.

Penalties will be awarded for:

- Head-on broom-bumping.
- Falling off the broom. (Extra penalties will be awarded where the GOer lands on a cat or a teacher. Penalties may also be awarded against the other side where the tumble is due to the illegal actions of an opposing team member.)
- Cat or bat deployment.
- Interference with brooms before or during a match.

This list is not comprehensive and the decision of the referee is final.

The Great Chimney

SATURDAY 6TH NOVEMBER

4:21pm Home

Just back from Ash's house and I've eaten so much there's a real risk I will **explode**. I haven't just been scoffing qurabiya biscuits all day, I've been *baking* them (OK, *helping* to bake them) and it's my new favourite thing.

There was an awkward moment when Mrs Namdar said I was very good at mixing the batter and I replied that it was because I'd been practising in Potions.

"*Potions?*" they both repeated, looking at me like I'd turned into a toad (I hadn't, I checked) and I had to distract them by 'accidentally' dropping an egg.

"We've barely seen you this half-term, Bea," said Mrs Namdar when I'd finished wiping up yucky raw egg and the biscuits were in the oven. "Have you been having fun?"

"So much fun!" I began to tell her about my forest expeditions, but had to stop before I mentioned flying broomsticks or said the *potions* word again. I really had had a busy half-term.

Ash didn't seem very interested in what I'd been doing. He was in a weird mood – not saying much at all.

"Is something up?" I asked him.

"*Nothing*," he replied in the sort of voice that definitely meant '*something*' but not anything he wanted to tell me.

I'll ask him again tomorrow when his mum's not there.

6:02pm

Turns out I *do* have room for ~~one~~ three more biscuits.

Very yummy.

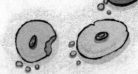

6:13pm

There's nothing nicer than eating biscuits in bed. If Stan was here, he'd eat all the crumbs. It's not fair that the class frogs have to stay in school at half-term. I miss him!

6:57pm

Just phoned my grandparents, but I forgot to ask if either of them had any useful memories of famous witches to share. I don't suppose it matters because I am one hundred per cent sure they've never met a witch in their lives ... EXCEPT ME!*

I wonder if Winnie would let me copy her History homework.

7:21pm

This English** homework is impossible. *Squiggle?*
Wriggle? Also, what is this incantantion meant to be *for?*
Spelling is HARD. *Gaziggle?*

I wonder if Winnie would let me copy her English homework too...

---

*Sort of...
**Incantations and the Language of Spells.

SUNDAY 7TH NOVEMBER (GOING-BACK-TO-SCHOOL EVE!!!)

11:05am Home

What I WANT to do on my final day of half-term is go back to the forest and muck about on brooms or have a proper swim* in Cauldron Pond. Or have another baking lesson with Ash *or* even just stay in bed all day, eating fluffmallows. But what I HAVE to do is get up and finish my homework.

1:05pm

This 'piggle' rhyme for English is still going nowhere.

SIGH.

*When I'm not wearing ALL my clothes.

7:55pm

Dad says I have to have an early night so that I'm
BRIGHT-EYED AND BUSHY-TAILED for
school. I've set my alarm extra early so I've got time
to make my own packed lunch otherwise he'll come
up with something ~~inedible~~ experimental and I'm not
risking school lunches again. Sir Scary Cook might
make the yummiest *magical* witchy cakes
ever, but witchy savoury food is NOT for me. (I still
have nightmares about those sausages, *yeeukkk*.)

8:31pm

Just remembered I forgot to ask Ash what was
bothering him yesterday. Never mind – he's probably
over it by now.

9:53pm

I can't sleep. I've got butterflies about going back to
school. I'm not *scared* like I was before my very first
day – when I was worrying about being bad at
drawing and Maths and the normal sort of

spelling – but I'm not exactly chill because literally ANYTHING could happen.

10:30pm

Wide awake, rereading my old diary and now I'm even less relaxed. I need to copy out my last TO-DO LIST because, well, I haven't DONE any of it yet.

Things I Will ACHIEVE This Half-Term

- Master all the trickiest **GO** skills including the Flying Cat Swerve and the Boggle Dodge.
- Persuade Dad to buy me a puppy (also ask if I can stay on frog rota because of STAN).
- Be the best vice-captain of the Dodos since the time of Minerva Moon.
- Find out who Minerva Moon ~~is~~ was.
- Learn to cook/make potions/bake.
- Ask Blair to teach me how to do the loop-the-loop on my broom.
- Levitate STUFF!

↓

MORE!

27

11:11pm

What if I can't levitate anything ever again? What if all my potions go wrong? What if I can't master the Boggle Dodge? Checking my tactic cards, it looks complicated...

The Boggle Dodge

Intended to scramble your opponent's mind to allow you time to get a clear run at the ball. The keys to this GO move are **nimbleness** and **agility**.

Twist the front of your broom handle first in one direction, then sharply in the other, flying in a tight zigzag to BEFUDDLE your opponent, allowing you to DODGE free.

11:17pm

What if I'm not allowed to stay on class frog rota?!

MONDAY 8TH NOVEMBER (FIRST DAY BACK!)

7:01am Home

I'll just have five minutes more snoozing...

8:37am
Nooooooo!

8:39am

"You don't look very bright-eyed and bushy-tailed, Bea!" says Dad with a grin. I think he's secretly glad I'm going back to school so he can crack on with writing his book. (Judging by the scrunched-up paper all over the house, writing books is very hard, but maybe he should have chosen an easier topic than Little Spellshire's *very peculiar* weather.)

I speedily crunch some cornflakes straight out of the packet and try to stop yawning. All I want to do is go back to bed. Bed is lovely.

"Don't forget your lunchbox." Dad shoves it into my schoolbag. "I made you a special sandwich!"

Oh dear.

8:55am School!!

I might still not know what I'm doing at Extraordinary, but now at least I know how to get there. I ran as fast as I could through the forest and I'm here with ~~five~~ four minutes to spare.

Mr Muddy is handing out copies of the timetable. It hasn't changed but he guessed that some of us might have lost our old copy/forgotten everything over half-term.

Mr Muddy was right! I had no idea where my old timetable was and tragically I'd forgotten pretty much EVERYTHING I'd learned last half-term.

Timetable: Year Seven (Form Teacher: Mr Muddy)
Student Name: BEA BLACK

Time	Monday	Tuesday	Wednesday	Thursday	Friday
09:00–09:15	Registration	Registration	Registration	Registration	Registration
09:20–10:00	Physics	Art	Chem/Biology	Chem/Biology	PE
10:05–10:50	Physics	Art	Maths	Zoology	PE
10:55–11:15	Break	Break	Break	Break	Break
11:20–12:00	Physics	Maths	English	Maths	Maths
12:05–13:05	Lunch	Lunch	Lunch	Lunch	Lunch
13:10–13:55	PD	PD	Whole School Assembly	PD	PD
14:00–14:45	English	English	Physics	History	Friday Lecture
14:50–15:30	History	Chem/Biology	Physics	English	Physics

11:10am

It's break and I'm doing some broom-cupboard-
bonding with Stan for old times' sake.

He was so happy to see me! Literally, it was the
best* frog reunion of my whole life. OK, he still looks a
bit gloomy, but I think that's just his
face because he leaped out of his
cubbyhole behind the grumpy
receptionist Mrs Slater's desk
and on to my head before I
was through the front door.
And *I'm still on frog rota*!
Which is a relief because I'd
been worried when the first thing Mr Muddy said
after we'd filed into his classroom was: "Right! Who's
going to take over frog duties this half-term? It's time
to give Bea a break."

"It's fine." I tried to sound like I wasn't stressing.
"I don't mind looking after Stan."

What I meant was: *Please, please, please don't
give my best-friend-frog to any other witch!*

*Also ONLY.

I held my breath as Mr Muddy peered at Stan. "He does seem a little less gloomy since you've been looking after him," he said. "Have you changed his diet?"

I shook my head (not if you didn't count the one-off accidental feast of fish fingers and far too many biscuit crumbs).

"Well, does anyone object to Bea staying on frog rota until the end of the term?" He looked round the classroom. "No other takers for Stan?"

There was a chorus of *nos*. I put my hands over the frog's little ears in case his feelings got hurt – what was wrong with these witches?

"Fine, that's decided then." Mr Muddy waved his wand like he was knighting me and announced, "Bea Black, I appoint you Year Seven frog monitor for the rest of this term!"

There was a spattering of applause led by Winnie and Puck.

"I suppose you have a lot in common," giggled Blair.

33

I looked at Stan in all his frogginess and he looked at me in all my person-ness and we both shrugged. *Whatever.*

It probably wasn't the right moment to ask Blair how to do a loop-the-loop on my broom.

12:03pm

Survived three periods of witchy Physics! OK, I didn't manage to levitate five objects at once in time to music like everyone else (even Puck – although he broke two windows in the process), but I *did* manage to levitate the tuna-and-toffee-popcorn sandwich Dad had made me up in the air and twice round the classroom! Such a shame* I lost concentration and let it drop into the bin.

Mr Muddy says he'll make a *levitator* out of me yet. Mr Muddy is a very optimistic teacher.

1:07pm

I've cracked Extraordinary school lunches! Avoid

*NOT!

everything savoury and concentrate on cakes and puddings. The dream!

Chocolate cake for lunch – *extra chocolately* witch chocolate cake. (Also a handful of Brussels sprouts because Sir Scary Cook insisted, but Stan ate most of them.)

EVERYONE is talking about the Grand Tournament. The Year Elevens are going to do a Synchronized Skeleshaker Display!

The Skeleshaker

So named because it SHAKES your opponent to the very BONE – the keys to this GO move are **strength**, **confidence** and **aggression**.

Grab the back of your opponent's broom as they fly past and ShAkEeEeeee as fast as you can!
Be warned: there is a fifty-fifty chance that the broom will panic and begin to shake back.

1:51pm

Eeeeuw, Stan is FARTING! I have a bad feeling the sprouts were a mistake.

2:46pm

English started out badly. Madam Binx has set us the IMPOSSIBLE task of learning the first *thirty-three* verses of the *Great Ode to the Winter Solstice* OFF BY HEART.

"It's not as bad as it sounds." She raised her voice over all our groans. "I know you all learned at least the first ten verses in mini-witch school." She flicked her wand and a stack of little red books took flight from the shelf behind her and dropped one by one on to our desks. I opened mine and gulped.

"I don't suppose Bea learned the *Ode* at her *Ordinary* school," sneered Hunter. Izzi and Blair sniggered and I went red.

Madam Binx glared at them and smiled reassuringly at me. "I'm sure you'll catch up in no time, dear ... and, talking of catching up, how did those half-term incantations work out?"

She was asking me? Oh no! I went even redder.

"Come on, Bea! Let's see what magic you can make happen with *words*."

I'd never managed to make anything even slightly witchy happen in English before, but I'd worked hard on my 'piggle' spell. All I could do was *try* so I shoved all my doubts away, closed my eyes, *pocus-hocus-pocus-focused* and said:

> "Piggy-hig and higgle-piggle,
> Make that witch's wand a squiggle.
> Try to use it, watch it wriggle,
> Higgy-pig and piggle-higgle."

I opened my eyes to gales of laughter. But they weren't laughing at me... *Blair's wand was wriggling like a caterpillar!* My magic had worked!

I'd SPELLED!

A second later, a gold star zoomed out of the end of Binxy's wand, transformed into a golden caramel and dropped into my hand! My first EXTRAORDINARY GOLD STAR!

So, in the end, it was the best English class EVER.

3:02pm

Blair's wand is straight again, but (not for the first time) she's not happy with me. I've tried to explain that it was only because her wand happened to be the closest – but I don't think she believes me.

6:12pm Home

Celebrating a (mostly) very good first day with yummy *ordinary** takeaway pizza.

*Non-witchy!

Great Ode to the Winter Solstice

by

Mistress R. Frost, 1766

Creatures of the land, lake and sky,
Come together to run, swim and fly
With witches from across the realm
Among the trees of oak and elm.

As witches gather 'neath the moon,
Each flying in broom after broom,
Join every creature round the fire,
And raise your mingled voices higher.

Although the winter wind is cold,
And snow is falling fold on fold,
Be you phoenix, dragon, bat or bear,
We have both food and warmth to share.

Welcome creatures green and scaly...

TUESDAY 9ᵀᴴ NOVEMBER

10:13am School

Mr Zicasso liked my worm portrait! He said I'd really captured the magical essence of my subject. I said thank you and didn't point out that he was looking at it upside down.

He was in a very good mood. "It's my favourite time of the year," he announced with a twirl of his paint-spattered cloak. "Time to make a start on your Winter Solstice masks!"

Winnie had explained the tradition – how at the bonfire party every single student would be wearing a mask representing one of the creatures of the land, lake and sky from the *Great Ode to the Winter Solstice*. Handmade masks didn't sound *that* exciting to me,

40

but everyone was cheering.

"There's card and scissors on your desks" (and suddenly there was) "and paint in here." Mr Zicasso opened a huge cupboard and gestured with a *ta-da* to the rows and rows of tiny jars of paint stacked up inside.

Two minutes later, we were all crowding round, *oohing* and *aaaahing* at the rainbow of colours.

"I WANT DRAGON RED!" bellowed Hunter, diving for one of the biggest, brightest jars at the same time as half the class.

"Calm down!" said Mr Zicasso. "There's plenty to go round."

I didn't know what colour I wanted, but not red. I picked up a glowing golden pot and peered at the tiny label:

PHOENIX

Oooooh! I weighed the pot in my hand. It felt strangely warm, but I wasn't sure it was the one for me. Maybe a deep dark blue instead? It would be easier if I knew what sort of mask I wanted to make and that would be easier if I could remember which creatures were in the *Ode*. Maybe yellow? Violet? Rosy pink? There were too many colours to choose from.

"I'll go for this one," I said at last, standing on tiptoe to reach a tiny pot on the top shelf. The little jar was cold and the paint inside was a bright lime green that reminded me of the moss on Cauldron Pond.

"*Hahaha*, perfect choice for you, **toadbrain**!" snorted Hunter, elbowing me out of the way as he reached for another pot of dragon red.

I didn't care what he said. It *was* the perfect choice. I squinted at the label.

FROG

Noooo!

10:45am

I've made a decent start on cutting out my frog mask.

If you'd asked me half an hour ago if I wanted to go to *another* Extraordinary party in any sort of frog costume, I'd have said **NO WAY**, but no matter how often I tried to put that paint jar back on the shelf it just kept jumping back into my hand.

At first, I thought I might make a lizard or a green bird or something else non-hoppy, but Winnie says it's very important to trust the label, and Winnie's always right, so frog it is. It's probably for the best – it's an easier shape to cut out than a dragon (like half the class) or a phoenix (like Winnie) or a bat (like Amara) or a griffin (like Fabi) or even a HIPPOGRIFF (like Puck*).

I'm trying to persuade Stan to pose for me, but he's not in the mood.

12:05pm

Maths was less fun. It turns out I'm still a bit *wobbly* on my eight times table. What a surprise. Mr Smith was very nice about it, but he says times tables are a core skill for all witches and he's set me extra homework.

*He's brilliant at Art.

12:15pm

I was walking to lunch feeling a bit useless when I saw the noticeboard.

Sports Notices: Team Captains

There it was, right at the bottom:

Year Seven: Dragons

Captain: Blair Smith-Smythe

Vice-captain: Hunter Gunn

Year Seven: Dodos

Captain: Fabi Midnight

Vice-captain: Bea Black

Even though Ms Celery had told me before half-term it was going to happen, seeing my name up on the board was still really exciting. I went a little closer and put out my finger to touch the lettering.

"Well done, Vice-captain Bea!" boomed ... *the*

board? I peered at it nervously and a little shock of silver stars exploded over me like confetti. "Bravo!"

I'd have fallen over in surprise if Puck hadn't been standing right behind me. "Congrats, Bea!" he said.

"Do you mind?" I asked awkwardly, worried he might think I was taking his place.

He shook his head and grinned. "'Course not. You're way better at scoring goals than me."

I started saying I wasn't, but then Fabi came over and said I definitely *was* and that the only thing that mattered was that the Dodos beat the Dragons, *especially at the* **Winter Solstice Grand Tournament!**

"We'll win," I said confidently because that's the sort of upbeat attitude the Dodos need in a vice-captain.

"Hahahaha! Not a chance." Blair swooshed past with her nose in the air.

I was the last person to criticize a witch for being competitive, but she didn't need to sound quite so smug.

"We WILL win!" I yelled as she disappeared down the corridor.

"Well, we'll *try*." Fabi is quite a realistic witch.

The Extraordinary: Halloween Term Winter Solstice Half Issue 3

Tournament Notices

- The countdown to the Grand Tournament (21st December) is under way. Get practising all those broom skills, witches! The Fantastical Flying Cup will be awarded, as ever, to the GO team judged by Ms Celery and Ms Sparks to be the very best one of all!

- In addition to the traditional GO matches, the tournament will include spectacular displays of tactical skills and hair-raising inter-year broom speed races. Ms Celery will be selecting witches to compete based on their performance during PE lessons.

- In light of the number of casualties last year, the parent/responsible-grown-up broom race will be subject to a speed limit of 199 km p/h. Students will be given a leaflet to take home reminding their responsible grown-ups of the rules of fair play.

- As ever, the tournament will conclude with a teacher/student event – the Magical Mad Mudder Race!
- Years One to Six will *not* be participating in the Grand Tournament because that would be a recipe for disaster. Instead, the lower years will have their own tournament, the Mini-Witch Games, on 13th December. Little witches are reminded that although not everyone will win a medal, everyone *will* get cake.

Other Winter Solstice Notices

- The ritual of Forest Bounty Day will take place on 29th November.
- Form teachers will notify each year group of the day and time when they should attend the kitchens for the annual Winter Solstice Log Magic Mix. Students are reminded that it is not acceptable to taste the mix before it is baked.

Friday 3rd December after lunch!!!

Quick-fire Q & A with Ms Celery!

Q: Favourite game?

A: GO with Cats of course! It makes the hairs on the back of my neck stand up even thinking about it. But any Extraordinary game is fun if you're WINNING!

Q. Favourite GO move?

A: Now that's a tricky question! I'm going with the Stealthy Slither – it's underrated, but deadly!

Q: Favourite animal?

A: I've a weakness for dragons. They're such fast flyers and wonderfully competitive.

Thank you, Ms Celery!

Dear Agony Witch

Dear Agony Witch,

I am DREADING the Grand Tournament. I am not at all sporty. I'm sure I'm going to come last in everything. Any advice?

Yours,

An Anxious Bad-at-Sports Witch

PS Don't suggest that I spell myself a sickie because I am a Hopelessly-Honest Witch.

Dear ~~Winnie~~ Anxious Bad-at-Sports Witch,

Your problem is you're used to coming first in everything! The tournament is only one day. I advise you to GET OVER IT and get into the spirit of things. You might even have fun!

Love,

Agony Witch x

PS Congrats on being a Super-Honest Witch!

FRIDAY 12ᵀᴴ NOVEMBER

11:05am School

First **GO** match of this half-term.

| DODOS: 17 | DRAGONS: 20 |

We were ROBBED – Ms Celery missed at least two fouls by the Dragons (Puck's lucky to still have four limbs after Izzi de-broomed him mid-pass like that).

I scored three goals, but my first attempt at a Flying Cat Swerve was a disaster. It started out well, and I was having a smug hair-in-the-wind-super-witch moment, but I didn't pull up on my broom sharply enough and ended up in a gooseberry bush.

"You need to work on your technique before the

Grand Tournament, Bea," said Ms Celery. "You're lucky you didn't have a harder landing." She picked a berry out of my hair and munched it. Just as I was beginning to think she was regretting making me vice-captain, she added, "But you *are* speedy – a bit more practice and you could be the fastest witch in the year. I'll be keeping an eye on you when it comes to selecting flyers for the inter-year speed races."

And before I could say *WOW*, with a flick of Ms Celery's wand, I was back on my broom and in the air and – oh no! – *Blair* was facing off against me in a race to the Great Chimney!

"*You'll* never be the fastest witch in the year!" she yelled triumphantly as she passed me easily and scored. *Broomsticks.*

The Flying
Cat Swerve

Inspired both by the shape of the arched back of a stretching cat and by their famously UNPREDICTABLE behaviour when left to pilot brooms alone. The keys to this move are **speed**, **precision** and the **element of surprise**.

As your opponent approaches, instead of swerving to the right or left, pull up sharply on the very end of your broom. Immediately, you will find you and the broom almost vertical and ready to soar up and over your confused opponent in a tight arc.

Bonus Move: The Flying Cat Swerve 2.0
Use the swerve when you've just passed your opponent, somersaulting backwards to appear in front of them once more as if by *magic*.

11:20am

It's very hard to concentrate on Maths after a tight match like that.

"If you're all determined to talk about **GO**," says Mr Smith, rolling his eyes and scribbling furiously on the board, "I suggest you answer this."

> If the height of the Great Chimney is 60 metres and GOer A flies straight upwards at an average speed of 2 metres per second, how long does it take GOer A to reach the top of the chimney?

"The answer is...?" he asks, looking around hopefully.

"Too long," chorus half of us (the half that are good at **GO**), but Mr Smith isn't in the mood to be fobbed off.

"Bea Black, put that diary away and answer the question!"

Umm... My brain has gone blank.

Winnie saves me. "Thirty seconds!" she shouts.

4:01pm

I've got permission from Mr Muddy to take Stan home with me for the weekends!

"I don't mind if your responsible grown-up doesn't," Mr Muddy said after I'd explained that I'd missed him* horribly over half-term.

If there's one thing I know my dad will be cool with, it's a visiting frog.

*Stan, NOT Mr Muddy, obviously.

6:33am Home

If it wasn't for the Grand Tournament being in a month's time, I would NOT be getting up this early, but I need to practise every broom skill I have – especially if there's a chance I could make the inter-year speed races. I'm meant to be meeting Fabi and Amara in the forest in ... *three minutes ago*.

This time I'm going to leave Dad a note that won't make him worry.

Going to the forest, DO NOT PANIC!! It's important school stuff and I'm going with ~~responsible~~ friends and I PROMISE I'll come home in one piece in time for lunch x

2:01pm Home

I've just bumped into Ash and he wasn't his usual talky-funny self *at all*. He wouldn't tell me what was up.

"Is it friends stuff?" I asked (because, when someone is that gloomy, it usually is).

For several seconds, he gave me the sort of hard stare that always makes me feel like I've done something wrong, but then he said no and shrugged. Before I could ask any more questions, the sun disappeared, big fat snowflakes started falling and his mum was yelling at him to come inside.

He's definitely stressed about something.

2:11pm

I need to come up with a CUNNING PLAN to cheer Ash up. What makes me feel better when *I'm* stressed?

2:17pm

~~Two~~ Three words: CHOCOLATE. FUDGE. CAKE. And the best place to get that in Little Spellshire (outside of Sir Scary Cook's kitchen) is Taffy Tallywick's Teashop.

Only one tiny problem...

2:20pm

Have persuaded Dad that this is a friendship emergency requiring an advance on next week's pocket money.

Problem solved.

3:55pm

Just got home from Taffy's and I'm wet, freezing and still very hungry for cake.

It all started out well enough – Ash definitely

looked cheerier when I knocked on his door and suggested an outing to Taffy's.

"We should go RIGHT NOW," I said.

"Um ... Bea, you've got that toad on your head again," said Ash, like that wasn't a good thing.

"Don't be silly." I rolled my eyes. "You know Stan's a frog, not a toad. There's a huge difference."*

"But you can't take him to Taffy's."

"Oh yes I can," I said, persuading Stan to hop into my hoodie pocket. "Nobody will even see him."

And before Ash could come up with any more reasons to delay eating cake, I'd dragged him out of the door. Ten minutes later, we were shaking the snow off our clothes and lining up at the counter of the steamy, warm, sugary-smelling teashop.

"Two of your *largest* slices of chocolate fudge cake, please," I said, grinning at Taffy.

"Bea!" I turned round to see Fabi and Puck sitting at the table in the corner and beckoning me over. But just as I was deciding to take the plunge and introduce Ash to them properly, Taffy dropped a

*Not sure exactly what it is???

teapot with a clatter. The sound must have spooked Stan because he slipped out of my pocket, hopped ALL over the room and plopped right into some random girl's ice-cream sundae!

"EEEEUUUWWWWW!

Is that a *toad*?" she screeched.

Her friends all joined in.

"Ugh!"

"YEEEUKKK!"

"Gross!"

Stan glared at them with as much outraged dignity as he could muster from beneath a melting ice-cream hat, then ducked as a spoon was jabbed in his direction!

Before I could do anything, Ash swooped over from the counter and scooped him up. "He is NOT a toad!" he declared. "He's a FROG. There's a BIG difference."

"Wait," said screechy-girl. "Ash, is that revolting toad-frog thing *yours*?"

Her friends snorted in a not-very-friendly way.

If they knew Ash, they must go to the **Academy**!

"Er, no." Ash went red. "Stan belongs to my friend Bea."

I went red too and gave an awkward little wave.

The group at the table stared open-mouthed from Ash to Stan, to me, to Puck and Fabi (who'd come over to stand beside me), and back again.

"Oi, Ash," said one of the boys, getting up from the table and looming over him. "Why are *you* hanging out with *them*?"

"Why shouldn't I?" Ash stowed Stan safely in his pocket and puffed out his chest.

"Because they go to *that* school, obviously," said screechy-girl.

"And because they're *weird*!" laughed another girl.

"Who are you calling weird?" demanded Fabi (who happened to be wearing silver flares and an even taller top hat than usual).

And that's all it took for everything to kick off...

Screechy-girl picked up an iced bun from the table next to her and hurled it straight at Fabi! Then, before

I knew what was happening, a cinnamon
roll flew right past my eyes and hit one
of the **Academy** boys smack bang in
the middle of his face, and a second later my
nose was nearly sliced off by a spinning round of
shortbread.

Taffy ducked a passing cupcake and yelled,
"OUT!" in the sort of voice no one from any school
could ignore. Moments later, we were all skidding and
sliding on the icy pavement.

"**EEEEUGH!**" moaned screechy-girl, shaking hunks
of bun out of her hair.

Puck was standing right behind her. "Shame to
waste them," he said, scooping up a handful of snowy
bun bits. "*Yum.*"

We might have been out of buns, but there was
lots of snow... I don't know who threw the first
snowball, but suddenly the air was full of them!

SMACK!

PLOOF!

YOW!! That one nearly took my head off!

Seven of them against four* of us – it was hopeless ... *or was it?*

Out of the corner of my eye, I saw Fabi sneak his wand out of his pocket and two seconds later a pile of perfectly round snowballs was accumulating at his feet at a terrifying rate. "AMMUNITION!" he yelled.

Puck, Ash and I snowballed-up and started hurling.

This was more like it!

Phut!

Splat!

Oooof!

Ha! They didn't know what hit them!

We were definitely one hundred per cent winning when the grown-ups stopped it – appearing all of a sudden from shop doorways and getting out of cars. Ordinary and Extraordinary parents, equally cross, yelled for their children to come home and, in the end, Ash and I were the only ones left on the street.

"Wow! Your friends are amazing snowball fighters."

*Can't count Stan.

(More *magical* than amazing, but luckily Ash didn't seem to have clocked that.) "Here." He retrieved Stan from his pocket and gently handed him back to me.

"Thank you!"

"Oh, it's fine – no offence, but I'd rather not keep him." Ash wiped his froggy hand on his jacket.

I laughed. "Thank you for standing up for us."

"It's OK. They were being awful – that lot always are." He hesitated and then added in a much more serious voice, "Especially Katy Snark and Brian Wurst – they're in my class."

I didn't want him to get gloomy again so I gave him the only piece of (squashed) chocolate fudge cake that had survived the battle and we slip-slid all the way home.

MONDAY 15TH NOVEMBER

8:57am School

"Your friend seems nice for someone who goes to the **Academy**," says Fabi as we wait for Mr Muddy to take registration.

"Ash *is* nice," I say. "You need to meet him properly next time."

Fabi looks a bit awkward. "Yeah ... but no ... look, it might be a bit risky. What if he finds out about..." He trails off. "I mean those that know, *know* and—"

"Those of them who don't, *can't*," I finish with a groan. That is one Extraordinary saying I'm beginning to hate.

"I'll tell you what was 'a bit risky'," interrupts Winnie, looking worried. "Picking a fight with

Academy students in the middle of town."

"We didn't start it!" I say defensively.

"Well, the whole class is talking about it."

"They'd better be saying WE WON!" says Puck with a grin.

1:03pm

Nobody's talking about a stupid snowball fight now!
Ms Sparks has announced that there will be a special
assembly on the **Winter Solstice Grand Tournament**
after school today and everyone is very excited.

Maybe they'll announce which witches have been
chosen for the broom speed races!
Pleeeeaase choose *me*!!!

4:01pm

"Ms Sparks has got on her Very
Serious Face," says Winnie,
looking up at the stage as
we all find our seats in the
Great Hall.

Of course she does! Even I know the Grand Tournament is a Very Serious Event.

"She looks *cross*," says Fabi, squishing in on the end of our row.

"So does Zephyr," adds Amara.

It's true – the headmistress's cat is glaring out from the stage with her fur all on end. *Wait*, is Zephyr glaring at *us*?

"Quiet, everyone." Ms Sparks is on her feet and clapping her hands. "Eyes to the front, witches, and pay attention."

I'm getting a sinking feeling...

5:23pm Home

Assembly is over, I'm back home and there aren't enough fluffmallows in ~~this house Little Spellshire~~ the universe to calm me down.

"A *bunfight!*" (Those were Ms Sparks's first words.) "Involving students of this school! A *snow battle!* In full view of half the town!"

I shared a panicky look with Puck and Fabi and Stan and, as one, we slunk down in our seats.

"I have nothing against a good, fair snowball fight among friends, but in the street? Someone could have been run over and – *worse* – I hear magic was used!"

Actual sparks were dancing round the headmistress and that was never a good sign.

"I expect those students involved to write letters of apology to Ms Tallywick ... and, of course, I know who those individuals are –" *aaaaaarrgh!* – "*but* I also understand that there was some serious provocation by students from the **Academy** so on this occasion I am not going to name names."

Phew!

"But something must be done."

Had I *phewed* too soon?

"This incident is merely the latest symptom of a much bigger problem. For too long, relations between the two schools – indeed the two communities – have been strained, with mistrust and prejudice on both sides."

Judging from all the fidgeting and whispering, I wasn't the only one wondering what this had to do with the Grand Tournament.

"It's high time I took action and the right place to start – as it so often is – is with the younger generation."

"You're not going to *t-t-tell* them?" Professor Crisp looked like he was going to faint.

"No, no," Ms Sparks said. "To fully reveal our *extraordinary* abilities to even the more open-minded members of the Spellshire community is not something to rush into. It would be too much of a shock."

She was not wrong!

"Let's start with the students of the two schools getting to know one another ... becoming *friends*." An anxious murmur rippled around the hall. "And everyone knows one of the best ways to make friends," Ms Sparks went on, "is to share challenges. A little bit of friendly competition never goes amiss and that is why I have decided to invite the Academy to participate in the **Grand Tournament**."

"*WHAAAAAT?*" shrieked most of the witches in the room. I didn't so much as squeak, but only because I was pretending to be invisible.

"I assume that no one has any objections?" Ms Sparks yelled over the hubbub. "That's agreed then. Excellent!"

"You cannot be serious!" Ms Lupo was on her feet.

"Ember, dear!" Madam Binx looked like she was about to burst into tears. "It's too risky."

"It's a risk worth taking for the sake of improving harmony in our community," Ms Sparks said firmly.

Now Ms Celery spoke up. "Well, *I'm* all for it." The other teachers looked surprised. "I agree with the headmistress –" now even Zephyr looked surprised – "'*a little bit of friendly competition never goes amiss*'." She jumped up and punched the air. "We'll beat those Ordinaries hands down – WANDS DOWN! We'll CRUSH them – they won't know what's hit them. We'll use all our extraordinary—"

"No, no, no, *no!*" interrupted Ms Sparks. "NO MAGIC!

That would be tantamount to cheating! We shall share the day in a spirit of friendship!"

"But ... if we can't use magic, how are we going to fly?" Ms Celery looked confused.

"We're not!" said Ms Sparks.

"Then *how* –" Ms Celery spoke very slowly – "are we going to hold an Extraordinary Grand Tournament?"

"We're not," repeated Ms Sparks. "We're not going to play *our* games; we're going to play theirs. We at Extraordinary will host an *Ordinary* Tournament. It's the right thing to do. The finer details are yet to be worked out, but plainly **GO** is a NO-GO, *hahaha*!" Nobody else was laughing. "All broomstick events are OFF. There will be no flying AT ALL," she said to a chorus of groans.

"Wh-what *are* their games?" asked a brave Year Eleven.

"I have no idea." Ms Sparks shrugged like that was a minor detail. "I don't think I was ever at an Ordinary sports event."

My headmistress might not have come from a witchy family, but it had clearly been *many* years since she'd lived an Ordinary life. "Races and things, I suppose. It can't be *that* complicated."

Assembly was over. The teachers, grumbling to each other, exited the stage and I was left trying to work out how to escape from a hall full of VERY UPSET WITCHES. Ms Sparks might not have named and shamed us, but it wouldn't take long for everyone to find out I'd been involved. Not long at all—

"BEA BLACK! THIS. IS. ALL. YOUR. FAULT!" yelled Blair at the top of her voice and everyone turned to stare at me.

"No **GO**, no broom speed races!" screeched Izzi. "No displays, no extra-special surprising magical events!"

"It's not Bea's fault," protested Puck loyally. "She didn't throw the first bun."

"If SHE hadn't been STUPID enough to turn up at

Taffy's with someone from the **ACADEMY** and –"
Hunter looked at Stan cowering in my hand – "THAT
FROG, none of this would ever have happened."

"That's not fair!" said Amara, Winnie, Fabi and Puck
together.

"It is though!" Blair insisted. "What a TOTAL
TOADBRAIN thing to do."

She had a point.

6:21pm

"Is everything all right, Bea?" Dad is peering at me
across the table. "Is there something
wrong with your fish fingers? Don't
you like the sauce? It's my own
recipe."

I shrug. The sauce is suspiciously
like raspberry jam and is actually
quite yummy, but I don't think I
could even eat witch cake right now.

"The problem's not Ash, is it?" Dad's
got his worried-parent face on. "I've noticed

that you two haven't been spending much time together recently."

If only we hadn't spent time together YESTERDAY!

8:11pm

Have spent ages writing an apology letter to Taffy. Stan has 'signed' it too with his foot (paw?) print.

10:32pm

No matter how many sheep (or cats or bats or even frogs) I count, I can't get to sleep. I wonder what sort of day Ash had at school. It can't have been as bad as mine – not even with Katy Snark and Brian what's-his-name in class.

11:55pm

Still awake (obviously). Maybe things won't look so bad in the morning?

TUESDAY 16TH NOVEMBER

8:56am School

Things look WORSE this morning. Everyone seems to have got crosser or sadder (or both) overnight.

"I wish the head had just punished us and not the whole school," says Puck gloomily. Fabi and I nod. Stan's nodding too. I feel bad for getting him into this mess – he's probably having a tough time with the other class frogs.

"I don't think Ms Sparks thinks she's *punishing* anyone," says Winnie quietly.

"Er ... cancelling the tournament? She might as well have cancelled Halloween and Christmas and all our birthdays at the same time!" Blair looks like she's going to EXPLODE.

"She's not cancelling it, she's just *changing* it," Winnie persists.

"Ordinary games might be fun?" Amara doesn't sound very optimistic.

"Not as much fun as FLYING," adds Blair, shooting me the most evil of evil looks in the history of evil looks.

Oh dear.

9:15am

Mr Muddy has a note for me at registration. Fabi and Hunter and Blair have one too.

To: Bea Black (Year Seven, V—C Dodos)
From: Ms Celery

In light of the ~~disastrous~~ ~~unfortunate~~ unforeseen changes to this year's Winter Solstice Grand Tournament, I will be holding an emergency planning meeting tomorrow. Assemble at the Sports Pavilion at 3:55pm *sharp*.

"Seems like they're inviting all the sports captains and vice-captains of the **GO** teams," says Izzi.

Everyone looks like they're about to burst into tears at the mention of **GO**.

"Bea shouldn't even still be a vice-captain," says Hunter meanly.

"Yes she should!" says Amara loyally. "*And* she knows a lot about Ordinary sports."

"I suppose she might as well make herself useful," Blair mutters through clenched teeth. "Now that she's RUINED the **Grand Tournament** for everyone."

10:07am

It's a much quieter Art class than usual. Even Mr Zicasso is subdued. Apparently, he'd had high hopes of winning the Teachers' Broom Race.

I wish I'd already finished my mask so I could put it on and pretend I was an innocent Winter Solstice frog and not *me*.

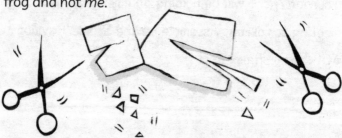

1:03pm

I should have had lunch in a broom cupboard with Stan.

"The last time they invited non-witches into Extraordinary," said Winnie, pushing aside her plate and pulling a copy of *The History of Little Spellshire's School of Extraordinary Arts* out of her bag, "was in 1715."

We all looked out of the big, arched window at the single crumbling tower that was all that was left of the original school building.

"What happened?" asked Amara.

"I haven't got to that part yet," said Winnie. She read on for a bit. "Oh!" She clasped her hand to her mouth. "*That is HORRIBLE!*"

Puck grabbed the book from her, read the same passage and promptly fell off the bench.

"*What?*" the rest of us chorused.

Puck held the book open so we could all see. Across two pages were written just six words:

AND THEN VERY BAD THINGS HAPPENED…

"Something *so* bad not even the history book wants to remember it," said Amara.

"Er … maybe the VERY BAD THINGS happened to the non-witches?" I suggested and they cheered up a bit.

"That was *practically* the Dark Ages," said Winnie reassuringly. "I'm sure nothing bad – well, nothing *too* bad – is going to happen at our tournament."

"Except something TOO BAD has *already* happened." Blair leaned over from the next table to butt in. "No flying at the tournament. No **GO**."

Everyone within earshot groaned.

"Don't witches play anything else?" I asked in a slightly shaky voice.

"We have lots of games!" Blair rolled her eyes and slid on to our bench. "There's **GO Faster**, but that's only Year Nine and up. It's played at speeds of up to ONE HUNDRED kilometres an hour. Can't wait!"

"It's dangerous," said Winnie disapprovingly at exactly the same time as I said, "Sounds fun!"

"And then," Blair went on, ignoring us both, "there's **GO Slower**, but that's just for mini-witch school."

"I miss **GO Slower**," said Winnie wistfully. "No one fell off and we never went higher than the trees, or faster than the cats, and we got biscuits at half-time. It was *lovely*."

I caught Blair's eye and hid a grin.

"And **GO Further**..." said Fabi, who was flicking through Winnie's book. "Except nobody's played that at Extraordinary since 1823 when two **GO**ers set out and never returned."

"Don't forget **GO with Cats**. That's the most dangerous." Blair grinned evilly. "It's only played once every three years on one of the full moons, but we never know which. Told you! *We* have lots of games."

But nothing, absolutely nothing that would work for an Ordinary sports day.

2:46pm

"I know we're all sad because we're not having a 'proper' Grand Tournament this year –" Madam Binx broke off from watering her giant Venus flytrap to wipe away a tear – "but poetry will lift our spirits. Let's have a quick-fire test on the *Ode* and see who's learned it all by heart."

Not me! *Broomsticks!*

4:01pm

Today has not been a good day.

"Don't worry, Bea," said Amara, catching up with me as I was beetling out of school as fast as I could. "Everyone will have forgotten by tomorrow."

WEDNESDAY 17TH NOVEMBER

11:00am School

It's only break and I can confirm that NOBODY has forgotten. Every time anyone mentions the Grand Tournament or GO or flying (literally ALL THE TIME), practically everyone glares at me. The only people being nice to me are Winnie and Amara – and *especially* Puck and Fabi because they feel guilty that I'm the one getting most of the blame. It's not their fault – they didn't turn up at Taffy's with someone who goes to the Academy ... and a frog. It probably doesn't help that I've only been at Extraordinary for a few months – I'm standing out in all the wrong ways.

"Don't forget the meeting with Ms Celery after school," says Fabi. *Gulp.*

4:55pm

Well, that went even worse than I thought it would.

"I've been doing some research into Ordinary games," said Ms Celery after she'd made us all sit cross-legged on the floor of the Sports Pavilion. "I must say, I was pleasantly surprised – they're more interesting than I'd been expecting."

A list started to scrawl itself on the back wall in her handwriting.

* Jousting
* Archery
* Chariot racing
* Wrestling
* Javelin

Whaaaat?? I squinted at the book she was holding: *Peculiar Sports Enjoyed by Ordinary Folk Throughout the Ages, Volume One.* That might explain it.

Reluctantly, I stuck my arm in the air. "Er, excuse me, miss. Except for the javelin" (and, for some reason,

the thought of a school
full of witches lining
up on the pitch with
javelins when their
rivals came to visit
was making me nervous)
"nobody does those things any
more. They're a bit *old-fashioned*. Perhaps Volume
Two would be more up to date."

"I can't find it. I think one of Professor Agu's
hungrier creatures must have eaten it." Ms Celery
shrugged. "Does anyone have any better ideas?"

I willed somebody to say something, but the only
sound was one of the cats in the corner coughing up
a furball.

"You'll have to help us, Bea." Ms Celery sighed a
deep sigh. "Up you come."

Aaaaarrgh! A flick of her wand and I was
hurtling through the air, landing clumsily beside her.
This was very embarrassing.

"We're all waiting." She glared at me (I was not in

her good books). "What *would* Ordinaries do for *their*
Grand Tournament?"

"W-well, they'd call it a *s-sports day* and, like
Ms Sparks said, they'd have r-races and things,"
I stammered.

"BORING!" heckled Blair.

"And high jump and long jump and, er ... other
races with jumps." My mind had gone blank. "Um ...
lots of running..."

"It doesn't sound very *special*," said Birdy Swift,
captain of the Year Nine Speedy Spiders.

"Well, there's the, um ... the three-legged race?"
There was a rustle of interest.

"Three legs, you say?" Ms Celery started to take
notes. "Is that a temporary condition?"

I tried to think of something less dangerous than
whatever Ms Celery was imagining. "How about the
tug of war?"

"I like the sound of that." Ms Celery was cheering
up. "Do we get to choose our weapons?"

I tried again. "Maybe the egg-and-spoon race?"

"An *egg* racing against a *spoon*?" Miss Celery looked baffled. "Well, it's not impossible."

"No, no, no!" I gabbled. "The *person* races while holding a *spoon* ... with an *egg* on it."

"*Why?*" asked at least ten witches at once.

I blushed and shrugged. Now I came to think about it, I really had no idea.

Things in the Sports Pavilion at my last school

Things in the Sports Pavilion at Extraordinary

Beanbags

Plastic cones

Hula hoops

Neat pile of sporting bibs

First-aid kit (plasters, antiseptic ointment, etc.)

Messy pile of unclaimed sports kit

Seven cats

Three broken broomsticks

Large chest of 'duelling wands'

One cauldron full of nesting blackbirds

First-aid kit (anti-bleeding spiderwebs, stop-moaning tincture, etc.)

5:32pm Little Spellshire Library

Nipped into the town library on my way home to get a book for Ms Celery that we definitely don't have in our school library: *The Department of Education's Complete and Concise Guide to School Sports Day Events.*

I had a good skim through before I borrowed it – it is very sensible and ordinary and explains everything much better than I ever could. PERFECT.

6:21pm Home

Ash has just dropped by with some 'spare' biscuits his mum baked. The news about the **Sports Day** has reached the **Academy**. "Are you excited?" he asked.

I felt much too guilty about having ruined the **Grand Tournament** to be anything as upbeat as excited so I just shrugged. "Are you?"

"No way!" He didn't even have to think about it. "I've HATED **Sports Day** since I was six and broke my nose in the sack race. Anyway, who has a sports day in *December*?"

"My school does," I said defensively. "It's one of our special traditions." Like class frogs and flying, but I didn't say that.

"Then why did they invite the **Academy**?"

I hesitated. If I told him that it was because Ms Sparks had found out about the bun/snow battle, *he'd* feel guilty too. "Er ... I think they want the schools to be *friendlier*," was all I said.

"Haven't you worked it out by now, Bea?" Ash looked at me sadly. "That will never happen."

THURSDAY 18TH NOVEMBER

8:45am School

There is a huddle of upset students and teachers around the noticeboard. "Tournament update," says Fabi, making room for me near the front so I could see. I should have guessed.

LATEST BAD NEWS

1. The Winter Solstice Grand Tournament will henceforth be referred to as 'Sports Day'.

2. The Fantastical Flying Cup will henceforth be referred to as the Fantastical Friendship Cup.

3. The events have now been agreed in consultation with the Academy and will include: 50/100/200/400-metre races, discus, javelin, hurdles, high jump, long jump AND the 4 x 100-metre relay race.

4. With effect from next week, <u>GO matches will be cancelled</u> and PE lessons will be given over to practice for these events.

5. Competitors for each year group's relay race will be selected following speed trials (time and place TBC).

6. It has been agreed with the Academy that competitors for all other events will be selected <u>randomly</u>.

GO matches cancelled! No wonder the mood was dark. And that wasn't the only thing witches were complaining about.

"Competitors chosen *randomly*?" sputters Ms Celery, jogging crossly on the spot. "Not on the basis of sporting talent? Honestly, sometimes I wonder if Ember even wants us to win."

Miss Lupo, Madam Binx and just about everyone else nod sympathetically.

"We WILL win!" says Blair fiercely.

"That's the spirit." Ms Celery cheers up. "We might

have to play their Ordinary games, but *witches for the win!*"

"*Win! WIN! WIN! WIN!*" The chant gets louder and louder.

"It's not all about winning." Ms Sparks has materialized out of nowhere* to join the crowd. "This tourna— **Sports Day** will include everyone and will be –" she looked around sternly – "a model of friendship and fair play!"

"Absolutely!" says Ms Celery through gritted teeth. "Fair play."

"Fair play," echo a few voices uncertainly.

Oh dear! I might still not be much good at magic, but I am *very* good at knowing when witches are crossing their fingers behind their backs.

11:05am

Professor Agu seems to be the only person in the school who's *not* talking about the tournament.

"Respect for magical creatures is at the heart of everything I will ever teach you." He twinkled at us

*So SPOOKY when she does that!

over his half-moon glasses. "So, until the end of term, I will be allocating each of you a task that involves the basic care of one of the more *everyday* creatures that live in and around Extraordinary. You will help to keep them safe and clean and happy."

"**EEEEEUGH,**" spluttered Blair under her breath. "He's going to make us muck out the class-frog cubbyholes."

"Caring for creatures," the professor went on, glaring at her, "isn't just good for them, it's good for *you*!" And, with a flourish, he picked up a long parchment scroll and a quill and started to allocate each of us our own task.

It *was* mostly cleaning – Winnie, Amara and I were on newts, Hunter and Fabi had to muck out the ponies, lucky Puck was responsible for bathing Excalibur the miniature pig and Blair did get froggy duties! In the end, every witch in the class had been given something to do, but there was one item left unchecked on Professor Agu's long list.

"Perhaps someone would like to volunteer for this *special extra task*?" He looked around hopefully. "Nobody?"

I hesitated – I didn't mind creature chores, but maybe I had enough on my plate what with trying to 'master' Year Seven magic and look after Stan *and* worry about **Sports Day**.

"Come on!" said the professor. "I know it's extra work, but I promise you that whoever takes this on will be doing their bit to make Winter Solstice even more special."

He was looking straight at me, but I looked away. It was too risky – I'd done enough damage to this year's Winter Solstice already.

"Bea Black!"

What?!

"Thank you for volunteering," said the professor.

Why was my arm waving in the air?!

"No, no! I don't think I'm the right witch for this—"
I began.

"Oh, I think you're *perfect*," he interrupted. "You can put your arm down now," he added with a chuckle (and, at last, I could). "I'm sure you'll do a fine job of looking after Egg."

Egg?

Professor Agu levitated himself up to the very highest drawer in the cabinet behind his desk and brought out what looked like the sort of ordinary egg you boil for breakfast.

"Er ... what do you want me to do with it?" I asked as he handed it over. It felt smooth like an ordinary egg too. Maybe it *was* an ordinary egg? Maybe this was the professor's idea of a joke?

"I want you to look after her." (The egg was a 'she'??) "Take Egg home and keep her warm and happy until Winter Solstice." The professor winked at me. "Simple."

4:10pm Home

Nothing at Extraordinary is simple, but I managed to get Egg home without scrambling her.

7:03pm

I've made her a little nest in my sock drawer beside my old diary. She looks quite comfy.

Taffy Tallywick's Teashop
No. 13 High Street

Dear Bea,
Thank you for your letter. Of course I accept your apology – it is all quite forgotten!
Kind wishes,
Taffy
PS Stan is <u>very</u> welcome in my teashop, but best to keep him out of sight of the other customers as I can't guarantee that they'll all like frogs as much as I do! x

FRIDAY 19TH NOVEMBER

10:55am School

That was the last **GO** match of the term and I am **NOT** happy.

Maybe if it hadn't been pelting down hailstones the size of puppies; maybe if the Dragons hadn't spelled their broomsticks glowing red and patterned with scales; *maybe* if Blair hadn't pulled off a perfectly executed Stealthy Slither ... *maybe* then we would have won. But we didn't. We LOST.

DODOS: 31	DRAGONS: 33

"Bea, a word." Ms Celery bounded up to me afterwards and I waited for her to tell me what a useless vice-captain I was. "I'm thinking the little witches might enjoy that egg-and-spoon race you were talking about – you know, for the Mini-Witch Games. What do you think?"

"Great idea!" I said. Anything to distract her from my performance in that match.

The Stealthy Slither

Perfect for escaping a tight spot or an overenthusiastic checker. The keys to this GO move are **flair** and **outright duplicity**.

As your opponent approaches you and attempts to attack from one side, begin to lean in the opposite direction and, as your broom starts to twist, grab tight and lean your whole body forwards against the length of the broom. Before you know it, you will have SLITHERED all the way round underneath your opponent's broom, emerging surprisingly and STEALTHILY on their other side and speeding away before they know what's happened.

SATURDAY 20TH NOVEMBER

10:43am Home

Ash has just gone back to his house and I feel bad.

Dad was out looking at clouds so, for once, I was doing my homework in the kitchen. I was carefully pressing some sample ingredients into my Potions exercise book and trying to remember the thing I knew I'd forgotten, when a voice behind me made me jump.

"What are *they*?" It was Ash, poking his head through the open window.

"Full-moon extraordinary bat beard and toadflax," I replied without thinking.

"Full-moon *extraordinary*—" He broke off. "Hang on..."

Two seconds later, he was standing in front of me and, before I could stop him, he'd picked a thread of the bat beard off the table. He *sniffed it* and said, "You learn weird stuff at your school."

Eeeek! I grabbed it back off him before it could do anything more than temporarily turn the tip of his nose green.

"What do you do with it?" He was way too interested.

Concoct a paste that makes salamanders fall asleep for a hundred days was the honest answer. "Er ... nothing much," I said.

"OK, OK, I get it," he grumbled. "You're not going to tell me because you NEVER tell me anything."

"It's not that—" I began.

"It obviously *is*," he said coldly. "You're like everyone else from your school – full of stupid secrets."

I glared at him, but I couldn't exactly deny it.

98

"Forget it!" Ash rolled his eyes. "I only came round to see if you wanted to do something, but I should have known you'd be too busy with Extraordinary stuff."

"I'm not too busy!"

He grinned a proper grin for the first time since he'd showed up and said, "We could bake? Or, I dunno, go to the forest and collect rats' beards or something?"

"*Bat* beard, **toadbrain**." I giggled and was about to grab my coat when I remembered the thing I'd forgotten... I'd promised to meet Amara and Winnie at school so we could get started on our weekend creature chores! (We hadn't even worked out where all the newts *were*, far less started to look after them.)

"Sorry! I forgot I have to meet my friends at school for a homework thing. Can we do it another time?"

I almost suggested the next day, but then remembered I'd promised to meet the others in the forest to show them how to do Ordinary races. "*Sorry*."

Ash said 'fine' in a 'not fine' way and now he's gone and, like I said, I feel bad.

3:11pm Little Swampy Pond, school grounds

Still feel bad.

There are a zillion newts in this pond. At least looking after them seems to be easy – just a few incantations to keep any nasty predators away.

6:12pm Home

Back from Little Swampy Pond and I *still* feel bad.

I asked Dad if I could go and see Ash, but he says I should have thought of that earlier and that it's too late to 'go visiting', especially if I haven't finished my English homework.

Write a riddle about a magical creature of your choice.
(CAUTION: Do not say the riddle aloud unless
you are being supervised by a teacher.
Anything could happen...)

9:23am Tangle Patch, the forest

It feels odd being back in this part of the forest without our brooms.

Amara is shouting at me to put my diary away. "Come and show us how to do Ordinary stuff, Bea!" she yells, standing on a fallen log ... that is the perfect height for hurdles!

Got to go!

6:11pm Home

Puck and Fabi and Amara are SO good at Ordinary sports! Winnie, on the other hand, doesn't seem to like Ordinary sports any better than Extraordinary ones.

9:33pm

Had a nice chat with Egg tonight about flying and friends. Well, I chatted – she just sat there in her nest, listening. I wish I could show her to Ash, but he'd only ask questions I couldn't answer. More secrets.

MONDAY 22ND NOVEMBER

8:55am School

Trials for the RELAY TEAM after lunch today. I've got everything crossed. Even Stan's got his (eight) fingers and (ten) toes crossed for me.

1:08pm

Everyone is trying out except Winnie. "It'll be fun!" I say, but she says that people have different ideas of fun and hers very definitely do NOT include any sort of PE.

For the first time, there's a buzz of excitement about the new **Sports Day**. The relay will be the fiercest race of all: *4 x 100* metres! The four best runners from our year against the four best runners from the **Academy**. *We have to win.*

1:13pm

"So," Hunter says, after Ms Celery had explained how the trials worked (and I'd explained it all again, *properly*), "today we race to find the fastest four runners and the fastest of the four takes the last leg?"

"Yes." I nod. "The person who runs last – the *anchor leg* – has to be the runner with the best chance of catching up if we're behind and bagging the win!"

"So that will be Blair then," says Hunter. "She's bound to be the quickest."

Blair looks up from tying her trainers with a double bow and smiles smugly.

"Only if she wins today," Fabi points out.

"She will!" nearly everyone shouts.

1:54pm

Except Blair didn't win. I DID!!!

It was ~~PANDYMOANY~~ PANDEMONIUM.

First off, there were *six* false starts because no one seemed to have explained ready, steady, go to witches before. Then, when we finally got going,

Hunter was disqualified for getting out his wand and spelling Fabi into a bush and we had to run again. Then Amara tripped over a cat and caused a three-witch pile-up and we had to run *again*. Third time unlucky – Izzi conjured up a cowpat, Puck splatted straight into it and we had to start *AGAIN*.

But the fourth race was magic-free and FAIR and I won it by a nose!

Blair, who'd been neck and neck with me all the way to the finish line, was NOT HAPPY, but no matter how many times she begged Ms Celery for just one more race, the teacher had had enough.

"Bea Black is last leg," she said firmly. "I declare her the fastest witch in Year Seven."

"Maybe in *Ordinary* races," snipped Blair.

"Fast for a **toadbrain**," grumbled Hunter.

"She'd better not let us down again," muttered Izzi. "Or else!"

But I'm not going to let them get to me and I'm going to try my very bestest not to let anyone down. *Again*. The least I can do after ruining the **Grand Tournament** is help Extraordinary beat the Academy.

The other runners are Amara and Fabi – and Blair of course. But *I'm* last leg!!!

TUESDAY 23RD NOVEMBER

10:35am School

We've all finished cutting out our Winter Solstice masks in Art and even mine is a recognizable, if slightly wonky, frog shape.

"Right, witches, time to open those paint jars," says Mr Zicasso with a grin.

I screw the top off my jar and *WOW!*

This isn't ordinary paint! It's ... well, I don't know exactly *what* it is, but with every stroke of my brush my mask is looking more like A REAL FROGGY FACE. It's like actual, literal frog *skin* and it feels like it too – damp and slippery!

Even Stan looks impressed. He keeps touching it with his frog paw and ribbitting!

"Look, Bea, I'm painting real feathers!" Winnie flicks her brush and accidentally 'paints' a phoenix feather on her nose!

"Careful!" Mr Zicasso laughs and spells it back to normal. "And those of you painting dragons, watch out for—"

Too late. Hunter's cape is already on fire.

2:46pm

"Professor Agu tells me you're looking after his egg!" Madam Binx says to me at the end of English class. "You must recite the *Great Ode to the Winter Solstice* to her every single night because nothing makes an egg as happy as poetry."

Seriously?!

5:43pm Home

"I'm *so* excited about **Sports Day**!" says Dad, the

second he comes through the door. "You didn't tell me parents were invited."

Aaaaagh! Of course I hadn't told him! The less Dad has to do with my school, the better. He might have his head in the clouds, but one day even he's going to notice something *peculiar*.

"Er, how did you know?" I ask, thinking guiltily of the invitation crumpled up at the bottom of my schoolbag.

"I bumped into Ms Sparks in Rhubarb & Custard," he tells me happily. "We were stocking up on fizzy skullsquigglers and having a fascinating conversation about the impact of heatwaves on toffee when, quite out of the blue, she asked me if I was coming to the joint schools' Sports Day! I said I wouldn't miss it for the world. You know how I love to cheer you on."

Dad is a very *enthusiastic* cheerleader.

"I can't wait!" He beams. "And it will be a good chance to meet some of the other parents and have a nice chat with all your teachers and find out what's really been happening in your lessons."

This is A TERRIBLE IDEA!

6:16pm

Dad is too excited making plans for **Sports Day** to cook (also, he seems to have come home with three onions and no bread) so it's takeaway for tea again.

"I can make a special picnic," he says happily, "with all your favourite sandwiches."

Oh no.

"And I'll need some little flags to wave."

Oh no!

"And maybe a nice big banner?"

Oh noooo!

8:08pm

Recited the first three verses of the *Ode* to Egg. I hope she enjoyed it (it's hard to tell).

WEDNESDAY 24TH NOVEMBER

9:50am School

Today's Potions recipe was already on the board
when we filed in.

- 1 gramme of finely chopped sacred
  earflower
- 7 petals of the moth orchid
- 1 medium-sized dragon chilli
- 1 cup of freshly made cabbage juice
- ½ tablespoon of crushed hepper peppers
- 1 handful of freshly dug mud

"Good morning, Year Sevens." Miss Lupo
waggled her wand and we were whooshed into our

seats at double speed. "No time to waste – so much to do."

A cauldron was bubbling fiercely and the classroom ponged of cabbage.

"*Motion potions!*" Miss Lupo took a sip from the ladle. "The sort of wand-work Mr Muddy teaches you may be all very well for getting things in the air and moving them around, but sometimes the clever witch will be after something more subtle."

She was talking at double speed too.

"For example, you might find yourself one day in a situation where a potion that either makes you go *faster* or someone else go *slower* might be the very thing."

She did a little skip.

"Can anyone give me some examples of when a go-faster potion might be useful?"

"Running away from a dragon?" suggested Winnie with a worried look on her face.

Miss Lupo nodded. "Of course, that's the classic example. Anyone else?"

"GO!" shouted Puck from the back row.

"We're not allowed to use potions in **GO**," Izzi tutted.

"Quite right," agreed Miss Lupo. "**GO** is subject to codes of witch honour, but there may be other occasions—"

"The Ordinary **Sports Day**!" yelled Blair before the teacher could finish.

This was making me nervous.

"I would NEVER encourage such a thing," said Miss Lupo, making a strange face.

Was she *winking*?!

"Let's just concentrate on getting this potion mixed and brewed."

She whirled round the room, handing out ingredients and watching over all our shoulders. "Excellent blending, Bea. You really are coming along in leaps and bounds."

I blushed, but I was really pleased because Miss Lupo didn't hand out praise very often.

"Right." She raced back to the cauldron. "Up you all come – time to taste."

There was an appalled silence as we all looked into the stinky green mixture, gurgling and burping in the cauldron.

Finally, Puck blurted, "We have to drink *that*?"

Miss Lupo looked at him as if he'd said something very insulting. "I'll have you know this is my very own recipe and absolutely *delicious*!"

3:00pm

I only had the tiniest sip and I'm still boinging around. It's EXHAUSTING.

5:34pm Home

I'm still *twitching*, but I think the potion's finally wearing off. I'll just have a little lie-down before tea.

5:41pm

EGG'S GROWN! She's nearly twice as big. I didn't think eggs did that.

Maybe it's all the poetry??

THURSDAY 25ᵀᴴ NOVEMBER

8:47am School

Rushed in to see Professor Agu before classes to tell him that Egg is getting bigger, but he says that's exactly what he'd have expected.

"How big will she get?" I asked because that's the sort of detail you have to know when you're hiding something.

"As big as she needs to!" he replied.

Eeek! There's not much room in that sock drawer!

1:56pm

The list of competitors for the non-relay **Sports Day** events went up during lunch.

"I've got javelin ... that's the one with the SPEAR,

right? *Haha!*" Hunter was ~~terrifying~~ happy.

Everyone seemed pleased with their events (I had the 100 metres!) ... except Winnie. She looked like someone had eaten her last fluffmallow.

"But you've got high jump," I said. "That's a good one!"

Winnie shook her head sadly. Apparently, it was NOT a good one. Winnie didn't think she was any good at jumping. Especially not *high* jumping.

"We'll practise," I said and for the last half hour that's what we've been doing (over any low objects that didn't have cats sitting on them).

If I'm honest, it hasn't gone *that* well.

8:55pm Home

They've been allocating events over at the Academy too. Ash has got hurdles and he's as down about that as Winnie is about the high jump.

"TOTAL NIGHTMARE!" he shouted across the gap between our windows. "Bet you a packet of skullsquigglers that I fall flat on my face at the first hurdle. I'm DREADING it."

Oh no! I was about to promise to help him practise too when his mum yelled at us both to stop talking and go to sleep. I'll tell him tomorrow.

9:21pm

Up late reciting poetry to Egg. I'm not sure when I'm going to have time for all this sports' practice.

TO-DO LIST

- Practise for my events by running EVERYWHERE.
- Learn another five verses of the *Great Ode* (and recite to Egg).
- Show Ash how to do hurdles.
- Go to school library and find a book on care of newts.
- Show Winnie how to do high jump.
- TRY NOT TO MESS UP ANYTHING ELSE.

FRIDAY 26TH NOVEMBER

11:10am School

"I am now an expert on Ordinary sports," announced Ms Celery in PE, brandishing the library book I'd given her. "And I can tell you that they are ridiculously easy – no Extraordinary skills required. No transformation, no summoning, no flying, not even –" she rolled her eyes – "basic levitation. Honestly, a *squirrel* could do these sports! You witches will have no problem winning every event."

And then she made us run round the **GO** pitch as fast as we could a zillion times. "Faster!" she yelled. "*Faster! FASTER!* We're going to **SMASH** those Ordinaries!"

I think Ms Celery is starting to enjoy this.

1:53pm

Professor Agu gave the Friday lecture today and
I now know that a wolfwish
is exactly 173 times more
enchanted than a goat (although
for some magic adventures
only a goat will do).

What I *don't* know is what
a wolfwish *is*.

8:10pm Home

Egg's too big for my sock drawer now so I've made
her a new nest under my bed with old T-shirts and
a towel. It's a bit dusty under there, but she seems
happy enough.

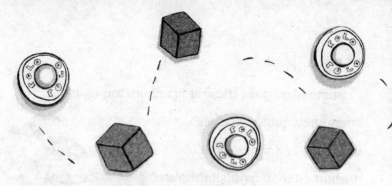

SATURDAY 27TH NOVEMBER

1:44pm Winnie's back garden

High-jump practice and Winnie's like a nervous pony, refusing to jump over anything higher than a garden gnome, even when I try to bribe her with sugar lumps and polo mints. Stan (who's come along to help and is leaping all over the place) is much better than her.

"Don't worry, Winnie," I say. "We've got lots of time* before the big day."

*NOT ENOUGH.

6:23pm Home

Just got home and it's very dark and Stan and me are frozen but, if it wasn't for Dad yelling at us to come and have supper RIGHT NOW, we'd go out again because Ash is practising hurdles in his back garden and it's not going well.

Ooops, he's flat on his face again!

I'll help him tomorrow.

7:11pm

It would be a lot easier if I could risk Ash and Winnie practising together. *Sigh*.

SUNDAY 28TH NOVEMBER

7:22pm Home

Today didn't go as planned. First Mrs Namdar wouldn't let Ash out until he'd done his homework, and *then* Dad wouldn't let me out until I'd done my chores and they took so long the whole day disappeared. Home chores are MUCH worse than creature chores.

MONDAY 29TH NOVEMBER

8:59am School

No lessons today!

"It's *tradition*," Winnie explains, steering me away from the classrooms and in the direction of the forest. "We never have school on Forest Bounty Day."

"What's that?" I ask, but before she could answer me Fabi, Puck and Amara have zoomed alongside on their brooms.

"Come on!" yells Puck. "Hitch a lift with me, Bea!"

9:32am The Secret Glade, the forest

So I did. All the way to the Secret Glade. (It's so secret it's never to be found on a map and is rumoured only to appear on Forest Bounty Day!)

3:46pm School

Back at school.

We're very cold and grubby, but we've collected armfuls of winter-smelling foresty stuff for the *Winter Solstice* decorations. It was like the forest was gifting it to us – trees lowered their branches and dropped great garlands of leaves and bunches of berries into our hands and no sooner had we taken what was offered than more appeared. It was *magical*.

5:55pm Home

"You smell of the forest, Bea!" says Dad, coming through the door, shaking snow off his coat.

Probably because of all the tree-hugging I'd been doing (Mr Muddy had told us that saying thank you to the forest with cuddles was a very important part of the tradition).

"We're decorating the school," I say, giving Dad a non-witchy version of my day.

"I can't wait to see it." Dad grins and gestures to the calendar.

One day is circled in red:

Sports Day!

"I don't think there'll be time to see *inside* the school," I say, thinking about all our work displays floating round the classrooms.

There'd better not be.

TUESDAY 30ᵀᴴ NOVEMBER

11:15am School

Our Winter Solstice masks are finished and we've been helping Mr Zicasso with the decorations. There are leaf-and-berry garlands everywhere and somehow* overnight the banisters on all the staircases have been transformed into gnarly oak branches that sprout leaves you can eat and toffee apples and sugared plums that grow back when you pick them.

I love my school!

12:01pm

Very nasty equations in Maths today.

I *mostly* love my school.

*MAGIC!!!

WEDNESDAY 1ST DECEMBER

9:55am School

Miss Lupo had something special for me in class today.

"I hear you're looking after the professor's *egg*!"

There was no need for her to sound so surprised...

"Well, you should have this." She handed me a shiny black egg-shaped pot. "It's ointment," she explained. "Just rub a little on her shell every night before bed – she'll love it!"

8:00pm Home

Ooooh, this ointment smells of strawberries. I might as well give it a go...

THURSDAY 2ND DECEMBER

7:11am Home

Woke up and peered under the bed to say good morning to Egg and she's got SPOTS! Pink ones, all over. *Eeeeek!*

8:35am School

Ran all the way to school so I could catch Professor Agu before registration. He told me to CALM DOWN. Apparently, the spots are "perfectly normal and nothing to worry about". *Phew!*

FRIDAY 3ᴿᴰ DECEMBER

9:00am School

It's our class's turn for 'Log Magic Mixing' later today.
Not sure what that is, but everyone seems excited.

2:02pm

Just made my first-ever Winter Solstice Witchy Wish!!!
I'd never been in the Extraordinary kitchens before.
They stretch all the way under the dining room, with
gleaming copper pans and bunches of dried herbs
hanging down from the ceiling and cauldrons bubbling
all over the place.

   Sir Scary Cook was expecting us. He was standing
over the biggest cauldron of them all, stirring
something with a huge wooden spoon. Something

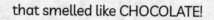

that smelled like CHOCOLATE!

"Don't just stand there like snoozy squiblets!" he boomed, gesturing for us to join him.

We stood and watched for a few minutes as he stirred the glossy, silky mixture. My mouth was watering.

"You all* know how it works," he said. "Everyone takes a turn to stir and makes a Winter Solstice Witchy Wish. Use yours wisely."

I knew at once exactly what I was going to ask for and, when it was my turn, I closed my eyes, stirred and wished as hard as I could.

Winnie says the next time we see that chocolate, it will be at the bonfire party and it will have turned into a GINORMOUS Winter Solstice Chocolate Log.

CANNOT WAIT.

*NOT ME!

SATURDAY 4TH DECEMBER

4:32pm Home

Oh. My. Broomstick.

It was so STUPID of me to practise levitating Stan with the curtains open, but we'd both been having too much fun playing keepy-uppy to be careful. We'd never got above twenty before, then ... *twenty-four* ... *twenty-five* ... *twenty-six*... Oooh, right up to the ceiling!

I don't know how long Ash had been watching before he shouted, "*BEA! Beeeeaaaa!*"

I made a grab for the curtains, but not fast enough. **"BBBB-EEEE-AAAAAAA!!"**

Reluctantly, I opened the curtains again. "Oh, hi, Ash," I said in my most nothing-to-see-here voice.

131

"You were..." He trailed off and stared at me like I was a hippogriff or something.

"What?" I smiled sweetly.

"*Stan*... You were making him go up and down..."

"Don't be silly, Ash!" I put on my most innocent face. "Frogs go up and down all the time. It's what they do."

Stan (who'd plummeted to the floor a bit faster than he'd liked when I grabbed for the curtains) looked at me and rolled his goggly eyes.

"And what's that *thing*?!"

"What thing?" I asked and then went bright red as I realized that I might have let Stan fall to the ground, but I was still holding my WAND.

Ooops. I could either tell Ash the truth or lie to his face. It wasn't a hard choice.

"Oh, *this* thing? It's a chopstick, *obviously*." I shrugged as if conducting airborne frogs with chopsticks was a perfectly reasonable thing to be doing on a Saturday morning.

"I'm coming over!" he yelled.

5:41pm

That went VERY BADLY.

By the time I heard Ash clattering up the stairs, Stan and I were sitting on my bed, casually reading a book. "Er, hello," I said as if I was surprised to see him.

"What are you doing?!"

"Reading."

"It's upside down, Bea!" He grabbed it. "*Ambius Ambrose's Animalium Magicum*?"

Aaaargh, bad choice. I tried to grab it back, but he was already reading aloud from the chapter on *How To Get A Dragon To Go To Sleep (& Other Basic Skills)*.

"Wh-*whattt*?" He goggled at the pages like an actual dragon might pop out.* "*WHAT* is going on?"

"NOTHING is going on," I lied.

"There is *something* going on."

"No there isn't." I wrangled back the book and chucked it under the bed.

*VERY UNLIKELY.

"*Yes there is.*"

"*No there isn't,*" I said, crawling under the bed to check I hadn't hit Egg.

"Yes there— Bea ... why is there an ENORMOUS EGG under your bed?"

Oh no! Why did he have to look?! *This was really stressful.*

"Now you HAVE to tell me what's going on," he said.

"*I can't,*" I wailed, emerging from under the bed, covered in dust.

He crossed his arms and glared at me. "Are we even friends?"

"Of course we are!" I felt all gulpy.

"We hardly hang out any more and REAL FRIENDS tell each other things," he said, getting up and heading for the door.

"*I can't!*" I wailed again.

"You don't trust me. You've made that pretty

obvious." He turned at the doorway and gave me the sort of disappointed look that made me want to crawl back under the bed and stay there.

A few seconds later, I heard the back door slam. Ash had gone.

That was an hour ago and I don't know what to do and Dad's calling me down for tea.

9:02pm

Still don't know what to do...

I couldn't, could I?

I *shouldn't*...

What would a good witch do?

What would a good friend do??

10:43pm

Can't sleep. I need to discuss this with Stan and Egg...

SUNDAY 5TH DECEMBER

10:41am Home

OK, I've made a decision. I'm not sure it's a good decision ... but I HAVE to do it. I'm going over to see Ash.

12:42pm

Dribbling dragons!

I DID IT. I TOLD ASH I WAS A WITCH.

(Several times because his ears didn't seem to be working properly.) He sat in stunned silence for what felt like ages, opening and closing his mouth like a goldfish, until finally he said something that sounded like...

"*Whoahhhaaaaaghwow!*"

And *then* he said, "I don't believe you."

Excuse me! After all that?! I should probably have thanked my lucky stars and not said another word, but then he said, "Everyone knows witches aren't real."

Well, that was just RUDE, so I told him all over again, starting with my very first day at Extraordinary. And then I got out my wand and made Stan go up and down until he looked like he was going to be sick.

"*Whoahhhaaaaaghwow!*" Ash believed me now.

I offered him a calming fluffmallow that I happened to have in my pocket and waited until he could speak again.

"I suppose there were clues," he said at last. "Even before yesterday."

"What?" I thought I'd been so careful. "Oh! The bat beard?"

He nodded. "And the way you kept calling baking '*potions*' and the fact you're always talking to Stan."

He looked at my frog nervously. "Can *he* talk?"

"No, well, I don't think so."

I'd come across bigger surprises in Little Spellshire than a talking frog.

"He can communicate with me in his own froggy way," I said and Stan grinned.*

"Can he do *magic*?"

"Not so far as I know."

It was dawning on me that I was shockingly ignorant about my frog. I'd never seen Stan doing magic, but that wasn't to say that in his own way he wasn't casting spells all over the place.

"Here. He's very *comforting*." And, before either of them could protest, I'd passed my frog to my friend.

"Why didn't you tell me before?" Ash asked once he'd got used to having Stan on his head.

"I *wanted* to but it's not the kind of thing you can just come out with. Anyway, we're not meant to

*Frogs 100% grin.

tell anyone ... witch's code and all that."

"Well, I'm glad you did because now you can stop avoiding me."

I was about to deny it, but maybe he had a point? If I had, it was only because I'd been so worried about him finding out!

"Is that what's been bothering you?" I asked, remembering all the times he'd seemed down.

He shrugged. "And er ... the last couple of weeks at school have been a bit ... stressful..." He trailed off, looking embarrassed.

Oh!

"You're worried about **Sports Day**, aren't you?"

Of course that was it! He'd told me he was dreading it.

"*Um...*" He couldn't deny it. "Never mind that." Ash swiftly changed the subject. "Tell me EVERYTHING about witch— Wait, what do you mean *witch's code*? You won't get into trouble, will you?"

It didn't seem like a good moment to point out that *he* might be in a spot of bother too, so I crossed my fingers and said, "Not if no one finds out."

"Well, I won't tell a soul."

He'd better not!

"Is your dad a wizard?" Ash asked a minute later. "Men can't be witches, can they?"

I snorted. "*Anyone* can be a witch. But no, Dad isn't a witch." I suddenly remembered how confusing I'd found all this and explained. "You don't have to be born a witch to be one. I mean, some witches have witchy parents – everyone except me at Extraordinary seems to – but you don't *need* to. I wasn't even the slightest bit witchy until a few weeks ago."

"What? You *learn* it?"

I nodded.

"Is it hard?"

The honest answer was EXCEEDINGLY, AMAZINGLY hard, but I didn't want to put Ash off because it would be nice if *he* learned and I had a witch-best-friend living next door. "Some bits are really tricky and some bits aren't," I said. "Like, flying's not hard."

"You can *fly*?!"

"Sure." He looked so impressed it was impossible not to feel a tiny bit smug.

"Go on then!" Ash pointed at the open window.

"I can't do *that*." (Now he looked less impressed.) "That's *way* beyond Year Seven! I need a broom." Before he could go and find one, I added, "An *enchanted* broom."

Ash thought for a moment and then said, "So, could *I* fly if I got on an enchanted broom?"

"Maybe."

"Will you show me?"

I hesitated. "You might fall off." He'd definitely fall off. Ash was not the best co-ordinated of humans.

"Can't be worse than hurdles," he said, so I promised I'd try to sneak an Extraordinary broom home next weekend.

That is if no one finds out I've told him and turns us into toads by then...

MONDAY 6TH DECEMBER

8:33am Home

The bad news is that I've overslept AGAIN.

The good news is I'm not a toad. I hope Ash isn't a toad either.

11:00am School

"You look worried, Bea," says Winnie at break. "Even more worried than usual. Is everything OK?"

I want to tell her SO badly, but I *can't*. Nobody can know that I've spilled the beans.

Aaaaaargh! It's dawning on me that I've swapped keeping one ENORMOUS secret for another. I'm going to have to be even *more* careful

142

to keep Ash and my other friends apart.

I HATE SECRETS.

12:01pm

Still not a toad.

Mr Muddy was very impressed by my Stan-keepy-uppy skills. He says when I get to fifty, I can have a gold star. I'd have been more excited about that if I hadn't still been panicking about telling Ash.

8:05pm Home

Just spotted Ash through the window. He's definitely still a person.

Phew!

The Extraordinary: Halloween Term
Winter Solstice Half
Issue 4

Winter Solstice News and Notices

Students are reminded to take every opportunity to practise their allotted events for Winter Solstice Sports Day.

- Ms Celery would like to remind every single witch that she expects to see them WIN!

- Ms Sparks would like to remind every single witch that she expects to see FAIR PLAY!

Further Notices

- We are pleased to announce that a new member of staff will be joining us next term to teach Geography: Dr Trudi Pellicano (world expert on caves, lairs and unexplained snares).

- Planning is under way for next term's Year Seven residential trip! More extraordinary news on that soon...

Quick-fire Q & A with Madam Binx!

Q: Favourite poem?

A: I have many favourites but at this time of year the one that springs to mind is, of course, the *Great Ode to the Winter Solstice* by Mistress Frost.

Q: Favourite pet?

A: I don't have a pet but I am terribly fond of dear Esmerelda, my Venus flytrap.

Q: Favourite joke?

A: I don't know any jokes so here's the first three lines of a limerick instead!

> *There once was a witch called Vavoom*
> *Who was terribly bad on a broom.*
> *It'd have been better by far if she drove in a car...*

The witch who comes up with the best last line will earn TWO gold stars!

Thank you, Madam Binx!

What rhymes with Vavoom? Kaboom? Zazoom?? DOOM??

Dear Agony Witch

Dear Agony Witch,

I think there might be something wrong with me. I come from a multigenerational witch family with many famous GO players among my ancestors and yet I've become *obsessed* with Ordinary sports. I think I might enjoy them more than the Extraordinary ones. I am so ashamed, please help.

Yours,

A Very Embarrassed Witch

Dear Very Embarrassed Witch,

This is *unusual* but nothing to be ashamed of! I would advise you to embrace this eccentricity. Just as some people claim to prefer other animals to cats, you should loudly and proudly declare that you prefer legs to brooms!

Love,

Agony Witch x

THURSDAY 9TH DECEMBER

7:55am Home

Still not a TOAD! It looks like no one knows.

9:05am School

Oh noooooooo! I spoke too soon.

SHE KNOWS!!!

"What's the matter, Bea?" asks Puck. "You look like you've seen an unfriendly ghost."

I am panicking too much to speak so I show him the note ... *summoning me to Ms Sparks's office at break.*

"What have you done now?!"

"Maybe Bea's done something *good*." Amara comes over and gives me a hug.

I haven't. I've done something awful. Too awful to even tell my friends (anyway, telling friends secrets was what had got me into this mess).

10:57am

This might be my last entry EVER because toads probably can't write diaries.*

    I've never appreciated how much I liked being a person until right now.

11:21am

FIRST ENTRY AS A TOAD

*Or anything else.

Only joking! That went way better than I was expecting.

"Ah, there you are, Bea ... and Stan too, I see." Ms Sparks waved at us to sit opposite her beside a roaring fire. "Hot chocolate?"

I nodded nervously and a gold pot on the table in the corner leaped up and poured steaming chocolate into a fat mug. Filled right up to the brim, the mug sprouted tiny wings and hovered carefully across to me.

"Marshmallows?"

Before I could answer, a flurry of mini-marshmallows appeared out of nowhere and dropped into my mug.

"As our first non-witch-family student at the school since, well, *me*, I've been keeping a close eye on you, Bea."

Oh dear. I tried to eat as many mallows as I could before she got her wand out.

"I've been having a little chat with your teachers and they all agree, even Mr Smith, that you're making real progress."

Progress?

"Ms Lupo tells me your potions are beginning to show signs of life, Madam Binx says you're developing a magical way with words and Mr Smith says you've even mastered the eight times table!"

Wait, *this* was what the head wanted to see me about? Not about telling Ash THE SECRET?

"Don't look so surprised, dear. I told you once you'd cracked levitation, you'd be off to a flying start, hahaha."

I gave Stan and Zephyr the last two mini-marshmallows and breathed for the first time since I'd sat down.

"Professor Agu tells me he's put you in charge of his egg too – that's quite an honour! He wouldn't hand over one of those to any witch he didn't trust to take really good care of it."

At the mention of trust, I started panicking again. The nicer she was to me, the guiltier I felt. Maybe I should just confess. "Ms Sparks..." I began.

"Yes?" She smiled at me. Oh, I couldn't bear to disappoint her!

"Um ... er..." I couldn't get the words out. "What's *in* the egg?" I asked instead.

"I'm not going to spoil the surprise! You'll just have to wait until Winter Solstice. Are you keeping her warm?"

I nodded.

"And talking to her?"

I nodded again.

"Good listeners, eggs." She raised an eyebrow and added, "*Very good at keeping secrets.*"

10:43am School

Ms Celery made us practise for the hurdles by running up and down the school drive and jumping over upside-down cauldrons. It didn't go well. Winnie fell over the smallest cauldron and Hunter (who'd clearly been at Miss Lupo's motion potion) was last seen running at about fifty kilometres an hour towards town.

I'm not sure Ms Celery still thinks Ordinary sports are easy.

Even Mr Smith is getting excited about **Sports Day**.

In the high jump, Polly Plum jumps 90 centimetres off the ground. Ralph Rizk jumps three times as high – so how high does Ralph jump?

If you ask me, Ralph is cheating *but* I got the answer right! My first gold star from Mr Smith! Progress!

SATURDAY 11TH DECEMBER

9:33am Home

It's snowing again and if I didn't think teaching Ash to fly might make him more confident for the hurdles (if you can literally *fly*, you should be able to jump, right?), I would not be getting out of my toasty bed right now.

10:31am Tangle Patch, the forest

"What's that noise?" asks Ash. He might have lived in Little Spellshire all his life, but he's never been to this part of the deep, dark forest.

"Werewolves," I reply and he laughs nervously. Probably best not to tell him I wasn't joking. "Ready?"

154

Looking at his face, I have a suspicion the answer to that is NO but, to be fair, is anyone ever really ready for their first go on a broomstick?

11:54am

It started off pretty well. Once Ash had given up asking me questions about 'how it worked' that I couldn't answer, I showed him how to sit on the broom, bend his knees and kick back with his heels to take off. With a bit of *wobble-eeek!-wobbling*, he was UP into the snowy sky!

But, just as I was telling him he was doing brilliantly, the broom started going *WILD*! It was bouncing up and down, and veering left and right, and he had absolutely NO control!

"Stay calm!" I yelled. "The broom can sense stress!"

I wasn't exactly relaxed myself – if anything went wrong, it would be hard to explain to Mrs Namdar.

"*AARRGGHHHHHH!*" Ash screamed as he shaved the top of a bramble hedge, did a couple of quite impressive aerial zigzagtastics and crash-landed into a tree.

Finally, his face popped out between the leaves. "Well, at least I landed," he said in a shaky voice.

I'm not *one hundred per cent* sure he's more confident about the hurdles...

SUNDAY 12TH DECEMBER

10:15am Home

"Where are you off to today, Bea?" asks

Dad, watching me layer on a third

jumper (it's freezing). "Forest

again?"

I nod and tell him that I'm

going with friends from school.

"Not Ash too?" I shake my head sadly.

"Can't you all hang out together?" he asks, looking

puzzled.

I WISH!

MONDAY 13TH DECEMBER

2:21pm School

For some strange reason, Madam Binx has given up
on poetry and is teaching us *go-faster spells*.

"Nothing like adding a tongue-twister to the end of
an incantation if speed is of the essence," she explains.
"*Super-speedy sylph and satyrs –*" she speeds up –
"*slurping sneezewort from a platter—*"

But before she can finish, Puck (who had the desk
closest to the window) leaps up and shouts, "*LOOK!*"

In seconds, half the class is at the window, oohing
and cooing.

"They're so sweet!" says Winnie, leaning out and
waving wildly.

Got to go and see what's going on...

2:41pm

I was not expecting that!

Amara made room for me and I looked through the fluffy snowflakes to see three lines of little witches in rainbow capes bobbing along on broomsticks not more than a metre off the ground. They all looked very serious and fierce *and they were all holding out golden spoons with EGGS on them*!

Awwww! Of course! Today was the Mini-Witch Games! "COME ON, YEAR TWO WITCHES!" Ms Celery yelled. "First three witches to cross the finish line get a medal ... and chocolate!"

Maybe it was the mention of prizes or *maybe* it was the go-faster charm escaping out of the open window, but all of a sudden the race heated up. Within seconds, there were speeding mini-witches jostling and wobbling all over the place!

It was CHAOS.

Someone had lost their egg! And another! And another! There were eggs flying everywhere...

Wait ... not a single splat...

Moments later, the frosty air was full of baby birds and feathers, and half the little witches had fallen off their broomsticks and were stuck, legs up, in snowdrifts.

"I NEED TO HAVE A WORD WITH *BEA BLACK!*" bellowed Ms Celery from far below.

Broomsticks!

9:55pm Home

Lying awake having a mini-panic. I do hope Ms Celery hasn't misunderstood any other Ordinary sports' rules.

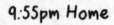
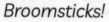

3:05pm School

More work on our motion potions today. We're
experimenting with adding extra cabbage, but so far
all that is happening is that Izzi and Hetty Hex had to
speedy-hop to the toilets to be sick.

WEDNESDAY 15TH DECEMBER

1:59pm School

Ms Sparks was very serious in assembly today.

"In just a few days, we will be welcoming guests into our school and I would like to remind everyone of just how important and valued those visitors are."

She ignored all the witchy eye-rolling, flicked her wand and a life-size hologram of one of my heroes appeared on the wall behind her.

"This man ran the hundred metres in 9.58 seconds," she said. "And he is NOT A WITCH."

"H-how is that even possible?" spluttered half the audience.

"'Ordinary' –" Ms Sparks made little air quotes round the word – "legs."

Hologram 'Usain' struck a
lightning-bolt pose and we all
applauded.

"And Mr Bolt is just one example
of an *amazing* 'Ordinary' person. People
who don't have – who haven't *learned* – witch
skills possess different talents."

There was a little bit of rustling and muttering, but
Ms Sparks went on.

"We may, for traditional and rather lazy reasons,
call non-witches Ordinary, but that does not mean
that they're not special, often brilliant. *Different* does
not mean less good."

And then she told us all about some ordinary and
amazing people like Rosalind Franklin and Martin
Luther King and William Shakespeare.

"Let's just say," she finished, "*there are more ways
to get to the moon than on a broom* and I want
you all to remember that, not only when you are
welcoming **Academy** students to our school on
Winter Solstice, but for the rest of your lives."

3:17pm

I levitated Fabi's chair* *and Excalibur the miniature pig* in Physics today! Mr Muddy says I'll be ready to levitate an ACTUAL, REAL PERSON next. I'm not sure about that.

*He was not in it at the time.

THURSDAY 16ᵀᴴ DECEMBER

10:45am School

"So, Bea, not long until Winter Solstice!" Professor
Agu is fizzing with excitement. "I can't wait to see Egg
again."

"You want me to bring her to the bonfire party?"
Egg might be growing and glowing and dotty, but I
couldn't really imagine her at a *party*.

"Oh yes." The professor nods so hard his glasses
fall off. "We shall all meet there in the moonlight and
we shall see what we shall see."

10:55am

And, no matter how many questions I asked him, he
wouldn't say anything more.

FRIDAY 17ᵀᴴ DECEMBER

8:55am School

All lessons have been cancelled by order of Ms Celery! Instead, we have strict instructions to get outside and spend the whole day running and jumping.

Fine by me!

Only four days to go!

This is not my To-Do List.
Oh, DAD!

SATURDAY 18TH DECEMBER

To-Do List

- Buy: pineapple, GLUE, raisins, sprinkles, MARKER PENS (NEON), sausages and GLITTER.
- Learn how to make sausage rolls.
- Finish banner.
- Make more flags.
- Wash and iron Bea's sports kit and whiten her trainers (how do you do that??).
- Buy Bea a new sports top to replace the one with the big hole in the front.

SUNDAY 19ᵀᴴ DECEMBER

6:23am Home

No time to write my diary. Must spend the WHOLE

DAY running and jumping!!!!

MONDAY 20TH DECEMBER (WINTER SOLSTICE EVE!!)

7:52pm Home

Dad has finally persuaded me that running round the garden in the frosty dark as fast as I can one more time before bed really isn't going to make any difference to Extraordinary's chances of beating the Academy tomorrow.

"You need an early night!" he says, making me hot chocolate to help me sleep.

11:09pm

Woke up sweating. Had a *terrifying* nightmare that I had to run the relay race dressed in a very fluffy dodo costume. It did not go well.

TUESDAY 21ST DECEMBER (WINTER SOLSTICE!!!)

7:32am Home

Something very odd is going on... I can smell something *delicious* cooking downstairs!

7:42am

Dad is making PANCAKES *from a packet!!!* Cinnamon-swirl flavour. *Yummmmm.* He keeps apologizing for not making them from scratch and I keep saying that that is *very* OK. They're warm and spicy and gooey and definitely the best thing he has ever cooked in his entire life.

"The weather in Little Spellshire never ceases

to surprise me," he says, leaning out of the window and peering up at the sky. "All that snow we've been having and now look at it – sunny, warm, light breeze, not so much as a dusting of frost on the ground. In fact, *perfect* **Sports Day** weather! AMAZING!"

Amazing? Or ... *magical*? I have my suspicions, but I can't share them with Dad so instead I say, "That's a very ... *special* jumper you've got on."

"Do you like it?"

It's neon-yellow with the words **Team Bea Extraordinary** written on it – front and back – in marker pen.

I do NOT like it, but I don't want to hurt his feelings so I fib and share the last pancake with him.

I need to hurry up and get to school.

(I think I'll leave Stan at home though – no races for frogs at this **Sports Day**!)

Plan of Extraordinary Sports Ground

Finish

8:17am School

I'm glad I turned up early. There seems to be a little confusion about the set-up for the long jump.

"It says quite clearly that there must be a sandpit for jumpers to land in." Ms Celery brandishes her borrowed library book at me. "Ridiculous health-and-safety mollycoddling if you ask me!"

"But not *that* sort of sandpit!" I wail.

It is HUGE. It's also dotted with sunloungers, stripey umbrellas, the occasional inflatable flamingo and wait ... is that a live lobster I can see?!

I need to find Ms Sparks and sort this out ASAP.

10:03am

The sandpit has been transformed just in time because parents are already starting to turn up!

There's not much mingling going on. Nearly everyone is grouping together on opposite sides of the running track – and even if they didn't have all that space between them, it wouldn't be hard to tell which parents belonged to which school.

The **Academy** parents have obviously been to sports days before. Their clothes are carefully chosen to match the **Academy** colours (grey and maroon), their picnics are in neat little cooler bags and their flags are all the same size.

The Extraordinary parents, lugging mammoth hampers bursting with witchy snacks, look like they've come directly from an explosion in a glitter factory in their sparkly multi-coloured cloaks. Dad's in the middle of them and, even though the jumper is making him blend in surprisingly well, it's hard to miss the massive banner...

Aaaaaarrgh! If I had my wand to hand, I'd disappear that at once.

"Is that your dad?" Puck asks me.

"How did you guess?"

"He's sitting between my mums." Puck grins. "It looks like they're getting on well."

Dad is deep in conversation with a witch with long, curly silver hair and a yellow polka-dot cloak. Judging by his happy face, his crazy hand gestures and the fact he keeps pointing at the sky, I'm pretty sure he is talking about the weather. The witch on his other side is wearing a pink feather boa and a tall, twisty, blue top hat and has exactly the same grin as Puck. She sees us and nudges the others, and all three of them wave VERY enthusiastically. Maybe as long as Dad only talks about the weather, everything will be fine???

Just as I was about to wave back, a voice behind me boomed, "GIVE ME TWENTY!" I was so surprised I dropped to the ground immediately.

"Not you, **toadbrain**!" Puck was laughing so much he could hardly help me up. "*Them*." He pointed to a whole group of **Academy** students doing press-ups under the stern gaze of their terrifying PE teacher.

I caught Ash's eye as he collapsed after the last one. His face was very red.

"Help. Me," he mouthed.

I'd have gone over to say hello, but Ms Celery announced that if the **Academy** were warming up with twenty press-ups, we needed to do THIRTY. "Put that diary away and get over here, Bea Black!" she yelled.

Help. *ME!*

10:23am

It's time to check the schedule. OK, the 100 metres is just before lunch break, Ash's hurdles race is straight after lunch and the relay is at the end of the day.

At the bottom of the *long* list of events is a notice:

First, second and third placed contestants in the individual events should go directly to the podium to be awarded their medal as well as points for their school (three points for first place, two points for second and one point for third) and the Fantastical Friendship Cup will be awarded to whichever school has the most points at the end of the day.

Good luck, everyone!

And there it is. On a red-velvet-covered table beside the podium, glinting golden in the sun, two gold hands sticking out in the place of handles: the Fantastical Friendship Cup!

10:40am

Ms Sparks has just given Team Extraordinary a final reminder that using magic is TOTALLY OFF-LIMITS. "I want you all to use your imaginations to get into the mindset of a non-witch for the day," she said. "Pretend you've never seen a wand in your life!"

That shouldn't be a problem for me – my wand is safely tucked away in my sports bag – but Blair is rolling her eyes so far back in her head that I thought they might go the whole way round. She sticks her hand up and asks if *non-magical* cheating is allowed.

Ms Celery shrugs and says, "If you don't use a wand, it's not cheating," at exactly the same time as Ms Sparks replies that it is most definitely NOT allowed.

"No wand-work, no motion potions, no go-faster charms – not even tongue-twisters!" This time Ms Sparks includes the teachers in her stern glare. "*And no ordinary cheating.*" She claps her hands. "Let's get today off to a fly— I mean a *running* start. And remember, what matters most is—"

"WINNING!" bellows Ms Celery and everyone starts cheering and singing some school chant that I'm going to make Fabi teach me before the first event.

10:48am

OK, the chant goes like this:

E-X-T-R

You better remember who we are

A-O-R-D

We're going to win, just wait and see

I-N-A-R

Worse than us you are by far

Y-Y-Y-Y

Better get ready to see us FLY!

GOOOOO EXTRAORDINARY!

No time to learn the other four verses because, if we don't hurry, we'll miss the start of the javelin!

"Don't forget your rainbow capes," says a Year Eleven, bustling up and handing them out.

Oh noooo! This makes Dad's jumper look ordinary.

"Do I *have* to wear it?" I ask, raising my voice over the hysterical laughter coming at us from the direction of **Team Academy**.

Fabi shrugs and slings his own cape over his shoulders. "It's *tradition*, Bea. Anyway, they're aerodynamic."

11:45am

There's a break in the schedule and things are going surprisingly well.

One of the left towers has almost no windows left and there are two spears in the fountain, but the good news is that not a single person has been IMPALED. Also, no magic yet!

In our year, Extraordinary won the javelin and the Academy won the wheelchair 100 metres and the discus. It turns out witches don't have greater natural non-magical arm strength than non-witches.

12:05pm

Things are seriously heating up. There have been some CUT-THROAT clashes.

Amara *nearly* won the 50 metres, but she was so startled by Mr Breakneck (the scary **Academy** PE teacher) yelling, "SILVER IS FOR THE FIRST LOSER!" through his megaphone that she turned to look at him a *millimetre* before the finishing line and a smug girl from the **Academy** took first place.

Hunter won the 200 metres though!

The **Academy** won the 400 metres, but that was ONLY because Puck tripped over his trainer laces just as he was about to make a glorious dash for the winner's tape.

It's close but overall the **Academy** are still *just* ahead.

The 100 metres is up next!

12:34pm

The race was over in a flash.

One minute, there I was on the starting blocks, next to *Brian Wurst* (hoping he didn't recognize me from Taffy's), the next minute, I heard the crack of the starting gun and I was off!

I was going fast. I was going *rrreaalllyy* fast. I could hear my friends and Mrs Namdar and (especially loudly) Dad cheering me on. I was going so fast, I was going to WIN!!

"Out of my lane, FROG-GIRL!" yelled Brian,* swerving into *my* path! I was so surprised I *stopped dead*! Only for a millisecond, but it was long enough. **Academy** had the gold!

I flopped on to the grass, dropped my head in my hands and tried to get my breath back. Extraordinary would just have to win all the remaining events ... except maybe for Ash's race...

I looked around and saw him standing on his own, looking really nervous. I had to do something to help. Right. I was going to risk it and go over and give him a pre-race pep talk. *Except* Brian Wurst beat me to it!

"Oi, Ash," I heard him say. "Remember which school you go to. You'd better not mess up the hurdles." He jostled him. "Or else."

I stopped and stood there, feeling *useless*. I was

*Broomsticks! Looks like he remembered me...

pretty sure that if Brian saw me talking to Ash, I'd just make everything worse! Was the best thing I could do for my friend to keep out of his way?

Wait ... maybe there was something else I could do for him. A teeny, tiny plan was forming...

Where *was* my sports bag????

1:02pm

They're lining up for the hurdles now. Ash looks like he's going to be sick, jigging around as if he needs to do a nervy-wee. It's not helping that he's next to Blair who is doing lots of show-off stretching. I catch his eye and give him a reassuring smile, but he doesn't smile back. I give him a big thumbs up – he doesn't know it yet but everything is going to work out just *fine*.

"Ready!" shouts Ms Celery.

"STEADY!" shouts Mr Breakneck...

1:21pm

The hurdles race is over. This is my HONEST account of what happened.

"GO!" yelled Ms Celery and Mr Breakneck together.

Blair took the lead straight away, zipping right over the first hurdle. But Ash wasn't that far behind her— *Aaaarrgh!* His knee bashed the hurdle and it came crashing down. For a minute, I thought he was going to crash down too, but he managed to stay just about upright. He kept on running, but he was wobbling all over the place.

I had to act fast. Blair was already over the second hurdle.

It was just as well I had something up my sleeve ... *literally* – because that's where I'd stowed my wand!

The next hurdle was coming up, the sidelines were packed and everyone was glued to the race. This had to be my moment. I crossed the fingers on my free hand, inched only the very tip of my wand out and pointed it, secretly, at the hurdle.

I'd promised Ms Sparks I wouldn't use magic to help Extraordinary *win, but I hadn't promised anything about not helping anyone else...*

One little flick of my wand, a muttered shrinking charm and … with an awful screech, the hurdle fell down just in time for Ash to sail over it easily. Not *quite* what I'd imagined[*] but still – SUCCESS! The only problem was that it made such a horrible noise, Blair twisted round to look at it and … CRASHHHHH … ran straight into the next hurdle!

Ooops. My bad. Before Blair could get up, Ash had steamed past her into the lead!

OK, it was clearly too risky to try and make the hurdles go *down*, so Ash would have to go *up*. Now was NOT the moment I would've picked to start levitating humans, but it was looking like my only option. I focused on Ash, took a deep breath and swirled my wand.

[*]Might have got the words of my spell a bit muddled…

WHOOOSH! Ash shot straight up into the air and cleared the hurdle by about a metre! His eyes practically popped out of his head, but he landed and kept running.

Next one – I swirled and flicked slightly less enthusiastically this time.

WHIZZZ!

He flew straight over!

And the next...

AND THE NEXT...

Ash was still in the lead and there was only one hurdle left to go, but *wait* – Blair was back up and gaining on him, a look of fierce and terrible determination on her face. I held my breath and focused all my thoughts. I had to judge this one *perfectly*.

SWOOSHHHHH!

Ash sailed through the air above the final hurdle, hit the ground running and broke through the finishing ribbon.

HE'D WON!!!

And I felt ... well, actually, I felt a bit *bad*. Ash was surrounded by cheering Academy team members, but he looked very *confused*. He should be happy! I mean *he* hadn't cheated. NOT AT ALL.

Ms Celery showed him to the podium and *veryyyy* slowly and *veryyyyy* reluctantly presented him with the gold medal. I whooped and clapped, but Ash was looking at me oddly.

He wasn't the only one. As soon as she got off the podium, Blair shoved her silver medal in her pocket and stalked over to me. "BEA BLACK," she said fiercely. "I need to speak to you – behind the Sports Pavilion in five minutes."

Gulp. She was one angry witch. Was there going to be a wand battle? Was she expecting me to DUEL her??

"You better be there!" She turned on her heel and stalked off.

Pretty sure I'm in DEEP TROUBLE.

1:45pm

I WAS in deep trouble.

Blair was sitting cross-legged waiting for me behind the pavilion, looking absolutely **FURIOUS**.

"You're a CHEAT, Bea Black!" She jumped up when she saw me coming.

"I'm not!" I protested, but I could feel myself going red.

"You made me fall over the second hurdle!"

"No! Honestly, Blai—"

"I know you don't like me," she powered on. "I know you blame me for getting you into trouble with Ms Sparks last half—"

"It had nothing to do with that!"

"I know you're jealous because the Dragons always* beat the Dodos."

"No! No, Blair—" I started, but she wouldn't let me get a word in.

"The **Academy** was already ahead. You betrayed *the whole school*—"

*Not ALWAYS!

"I didn't—"

"And *I* haven't cheated once today even though I REALLY wanted to and even though I'm pretty sure some of the **Academy** have been cheating. Gerty Twistle says she thinks they've been contestant swapping in the Year Eleven discus."

"No!"

Blair nodded wide-eyed, but then remembered she was angry with *me*. "You're no better than them! If *I'd* used magic, I'd have used it to help Extraordinary. And I'd have come up with something better than a simple distraction-and-tripwire charm."

What was she talking about?

"I promise I didn't mean for you to trip up. It was a complete accident."

"Stop lying! I saw you use your WAND."

I took a deep breath. "Yes I did. I *was* cheating and I'm *sorry* – but I wasn't trying to make you lose. I was just trying to make my friend Ash win. I wanted to shrink the first hurdle, but it fell over instead and made this horrible screeching noise and then—"

"So that noise wasn't a distraction?" Blair frowned. "And there was no magical tripwire? I just actually tripped over a hurdle? *Me?* I fell over?"

"Um..." I wasn't sure how she wanted me to answer that. "Er ... yes?"

Blair stared hard at me for a minute without saying anything. "You did it for your friend, you say?" Was her voice friendlier? "Maybe you'll make a witch yet, but this doesn't mean that I forgive you, right?" I nodded. "And it doesn't mean that I won't get my revenge one day."

Oh dear.

"But I am prepared to let it go for today ... on ONE condition."

"Name it," I replied – and immediately regretted it.

"From now on," Blair continued with a terrifying grin, "ANYTHING GOES." And, without waiting for an answer, she was sprinting off back to the pitches like a dragon was on her tail!

"Uhhhh, Blair," I called after her. "What do you mean by *anything*?" But she was already too far away.

"*Contestants in the Year Seven long jump must proceed to the sandpit NOW*," Ms Celery's voice is blaring over the loudspeaker.

Amara and Puck are in that event – got to go...

2:21pm

I was just in time to see the start. Puck jumped first and it was a good jump, but the Academy girl that jumped next got even further. Except  for the fact that several of the Extraordinary parents were now wearing the brand-new sports cones as hats, everything seemed quite normal. Amara was up next. It was probably a mistake for me to yell, "GO, AMARA!" quite as loudly as I did because she messed up her take-off so badly she barely took off at all.

"*Extraordinary!*" sniggered Mr Breakneck. Ms Celery put her head in her hands and groaned.

Next went two more competitors from the Academy. They sailed past Puck's marker by miles.* We were getting trashed. Izzi Geronimo was our last contender and she wasn't even our best jumper.

I glanced over at Blair, but she didn't seem worried at all.

Izzi stepped up to the line, took her three paces back and started her run-up.

I looked back to Blair and noticed she was muttering something under her breath... At the very moment Izzi jumped, the ground under her feet sank, then pinged back like a trampoline!

WHIIIIIIZZZZZ!

Izzi flew through the air, arms and legs flailing. She flew easily over all the other little flag markers; she flew straight past Mr Breakneck; she flew out over the end of the HUGE landing sandpit!

The crowd gasped. Even the watching school cats gasped.

*31 and 37 centimetres to be precise.

WHAM! Finally, she landed in a big pile of leaves someone had raked off the running track.

A Year Ten Extraordinary with a clipboard and a measuring tape ran forwards. "Seventeen metres!" he yelled.

Mr Breakneck's eyes practically popped out of his head. "*That-that-that* can't be right," he stuttered. "That's nearly *double the world record.*"

"Well, well, well!" Ms Celery might be looking surprised, but she was also looking VERY smug.

2:40pm

High jump next and Winnie was first to go. She was shaking like a jelly but, before she even started her run-up, a little gust of wind was making our rainbow cloaks billow and, by the time she lifted off, it had turned into a *micro-tornado* that sent her flying up,

193

up, *up* into the air ... and *farrrrrrr* over the high-jump bar. She did a little somersault in the sky and then plopped back down on to the mat.

Broomsticks!

"Two point two metres! *Excellent*," Ms Celery grinned.

The Extraordinary spectators whooped, Winnie looked completely baffled, the Academy spectators groaned and gasped. Ms Celery and Blair were jumping up and down and clapping wildly.

The bar was raised again and again ... and *again*, until it was at the highest rung. Again and again and again, Winnie whizzed over.

"Two point five metres! *Extraordinary*," crowed Ms Celery.

But, before I could join the crush of witches congratulating Winnie, a voice behind me said, "Bea. Black. I. Need. To. Speak. To. You. NOW!"

Not again!

2:55pm

Writing down what happened next is PAINFUL... For the second time in an hour, I was back behind the pavilion with someone who was very angry with me. But this time it wasn't Blair – it was *Ash*.

"Um ... is something wrong?" I asked, trying and failing to smile innocently.

"You know exactly what's wrong, Bea – I've never hurdled ... I've never even *jumped* like that in my life." He glared at me.

"But you *did* hurdle like that!" I protested.

"Come on!" Ash looked at me in that I-can-see-through-you way and I went so red it's a wonder I didn't burst into flames. "Be honest with me, Bea ... for once."

Ouch.

"I-I-I d-didn't mean ... I just thought—"

"What? *What?* That I needed help? Because I'm not as good at sport as you?"

"No!" Well, *sort of* but there had to be a better way of putting it. "I didn't want you to have a horrible **Sports Day**. I wanted you to *win*."

"By making me into a *cheat*?!"

"You didn't cheat!"

"No, but *you* did and I didn't win this fair and square."

Ash pulled the medal ribbon over his head. "Here, you have it. You won it." He tossed it, glinting gold, high into the tangly branches of a nearby tree.

I started to climb up after it. "I was trying to help," I called down. "I knew you were stressed about your race."

"*I don't care about races.*"

"Then what?" I didn't understand.

"You have no idea, do you?"

I clung from a branch like a monkey and yelled down. "TELL ME!"

There was a long moment as we looked at each other and then he blurted it out. "Well, if you really want to know, Bea, it SUCKS being the only person at my school who's friends with someone from your school … and a *frog*."

What?

"Brian and Katy told everyone at school what happened at Taffy's."

Now he'd started, it was all coming out.

"Half my class started calling me FROG BOY!"

They'd been being mean to him all this time because of *me*!

"But I stayed your friend … even though *you* were always busy with your secrets and your *witch* friends."

Whaaaaaat?

"But Ash!" I peered through the leaves in shock. "You should have told me. If I'd known, I wouldn't just have magicked the hurdles. I'd have—"

"What, Bea?" he yelled. "You'd have waved your WAND again? Do you really think that would have helped?" He started to walk away.

"*Waaait!*" I called but, by the time I'd untangled myself from the branches and scrambled down, Ash had gone.

4:11pm Home

I wish I'd run after him straight away because when I did make it back to the pitch, Ms Celery was looking for me.

"Come on, Bea! If you miss the start, we'll be disqualified!" she shrieked.

The relay!

My head was so all over the place I wasn't even sure I could remember how to run, but I let her drag me to my starting place. I looked across the track and Blair winked at me, which did NOT calm me down.

BANG! went the starting gun and...

"Go EXTRAAAAORDDDINAAAARY!" yelled Dad.

"False start!" called Mr Breakneck. I was now VERY NOT CALM.

BANG! went the starting gun again and the first runners were off!

"Go Amara!" I heard all the Extraordinaries yell.

But just as I was trying to persuade myself that everything – in the race at least – was going to be *fine*, I heard a buzzing sound. It was faint at first, but it

kept getting louder and louder. It sounded like it was coming from my right? No, my left? My right *and* my left???

I ducked just in time as a massive swarm of *BEES* zipped past me and across the track. They were making for the **Academy** runner out in front!

"*ARRRRGGHH!*" she screamed as the bees dive-bombed towards her. She dodged one way, then the other, veering around in zigzags. She did well staying on track, but by the time she handed over to their second leg (and the bees had spiralled away into the trees) Fabi had the baton and Extraordinary were way ahead!

Oh no! The next **Academy** runner wasn't faring much better. A glittery rainbow cloak had appeared out of nowhere and wrapped him up like a mummy. "I can't SEEEEEEE!!!!" he wailed as he ran straight off the track and plunged HEAD FIRST into the crowd of spectators!

Blair was already taking the baton from Fabi. Even from across the track I could see how wildly it was shaking and shuddering. Then there was a strange sort of *fizzing* sound, a skitter of red sparky flames burst out of the baton and Blair started running faster than I'd ever seen her run before! Her legs were all blurry and her feet were hardly even touching the ground, like she was being propelled by something ... and she was coming my way!

I looked for Ms Sparks on the sidelines. If I'd noticed Blair's *rocket-baton*, surely she had? But Ms Sparks wasn't looking at Blair. Instead, she was looking up at the sky...

An instant later, I felt a thick *snowflake* hit my arm, then another, then another. Within seconds, the snow was coming thick and fast, swirling through the air and settling in heaps across the track.

NEVER had WEATHER happened so *FAST*!

Forget the relay, some of the parents were already beginning to run for cover. Dad, on the other hand, pulling out his notebook and pencil, looked more excited than ever. There was snow everywhere now – on my shoulders, in my eyelashes, piling up on top of my head. Blair was snowed so far under that she couldn't move her feet to run any more and the rocket-baton had fizzled out in its own little snowdrift.

"OH DEAR!" shouted Ms Sparks into her megaphone. "Looks like we'll have to end the race there. What a *shame*. EVERYONE TO THE GREAT TENT."

I grabbed Dad (who would have stared at the snowstorm until he turned into an actual snowman) and ran towards the tent.

Inside, it was all warm and cosy. Sir Scary Cook had laid out a mammoth feast under two banners helpfully labelled *ORDINARY Savoury Stuff* and *EXTRAORDINARY Sweet Things*.

The strangest thing was that, for the first time that day, the Ordinaries and the Extraordinaries were *actually MINGLING*, dusting the snow off each others' heads and marvelling at how *'even for Little Spellshire, this was strange weather'*. And some of the students were actually talking to each other!

The friendly mood made me want to find Ash

more than ever. I hadn't seen him in the crowd at the relay. I craned my neck, but I couldn't see him or Mrs Namdar anywhere.

Before I could look properly, there was a cough from the front of the room – Ms Sparks was holding a megaphone. "Hello, everyone, witch— er, *watchers* and spectators. I would like to thank you *all* for coming today. It has been lovely to welcome you to our school. Because of the *tragic* and ENTIRELY UNEXPECTED turn in the weather, the official score is a *draw*."

Mr Breakneck and Ms Celery glared at each other.

"BUT," Ms Sparks continued, "as the **Academy** are our guests and in light of some ... *unsportsmanlike conduct* on the part of Extraordinary students, I will be awarding the Fantastical Friendship Cup to the ACADEMY!" The **Academy** parents and students started cheering and whooping and even the Extraordinaries, now they were warm and inside and standing next to the Ordinaries, couldn't help clapping along too. There would always be *next year*, I heard more than one person say.

I looked over at Blair and even she didn't look angry. But then we were both very lucky not to have been immediately exSPELLED and/or have other VERY BAD THINGS happen to us.

I still couldn't see Ash anywhere, but I found Dad gulping down triple chocolate biscuits.

"There you are, Bea!" he said and started to tell me how proud he was of me even though I hadn't won any of my races.

"Never mind that," I interrupted. "Have you seen Ash?" But he hadn't – no one seemed to know where he was.

Aaaargh! I jumped in the air – Ms Sparks had crept up on me and tapped me on the shoulder.

"Bea," she said and I waited for the telling-off I deserved. "If by any chance you're looking for your friend from the **Academy**, I do believe he's gone home."

How did she always know everything?!

"Don't just stand there gawping at me – if I were you, I'd run after him and sort things out." She patted me briskly on the arm and added, "Friendships are a bit like *eggs* you know, Bea. They can be *fragile*. Best to look after them carefully."

4:45pm Ash's house

"Oh, hello, Bea dear." Mrs Namdar looked a little flustered. "And … your frog." (I'd told Stan everything and he'd come with me for moral support.)

"Can I come in and see Ash?"

"Er… He's busy with his homework," she ~~said~~ lied.

5:01pm Ash's house (again)

Mrs Namdar looked surprised to see me standing on the doorstep again so soon.

"Has he finished his homework?" I asked.

"Go away!" Ash shouted from somewhere behind her.

"Probably best to pop back tomorrow?" said Mrs Namdar awkwardly, thrusting a still-warm-from-the-oven raisin biscuit into my hand to soften the blow.

5:12pm Ash's house (AGAIN!)

"WHAT DO YOU WANT?" This time it was Ash who opened the door.

"To say sorry," I said in a very small voice. "*Please.*"

He let me and Stan come in, but *very* reluctantly. I followed him into the kitchen and Mrs Namdar, without saying a word, handed me a whole plate of biscuits and disappeared.

6:01pm

We talked for ages and at first it was *awful*, but then it got better.

I said sorry for the hurdles disaster and being an awful friend about a zillion times until Ash ended up

yelling at me to STOP APOLOGIZING. So I did because
he was really quite scary. And then *he* started
apologizing for saying that it sucked being
friends with me and Stan, and *I* had to yell at
him until he stopped. It was exhausting and
we had to eat all of Mrs Namdar's biscuits
to recover.

"Do you *promise* you won't do magic on
me again?" he asked when the plate was empty
and Stan had hoovered up every last crumb.

"I promise," I said. "But *pleeease* can I do magic
on Brian Wurst and Katy what's-her-name?" It was
such a shame I didn't know how to do a turning-into-
a-worm spell, but I was sure I could come up with
something.

"No," said Ash. "Not even on them. There are worse
names to be called at school than Frog Boy." (Stan
nodded.) "I'm sorting things out myself. I don't want
you to do magic *on* me and I don't want you to do
magic *for* me."

I thought I understood. "OK." I nodded. "I'll teach

you to do magic."

"NO! I want to handle things my own way and that means NO MAGIC."

Whaaat?

Ash looked at my face and laughed. "None. I mean it!"

No magic at all? Not even a teeny-tiny charm or a drop of potions?

"Not even flying?" I gasped.

"Especially not flying!"

"B-but—"

"I'm OK with *you* doing magic," said Ash kindly. "I think it's cool and I'm glad you told me."

I was glad too (except for the stress dreams about being turned into a toad).

"But it's not for me, Bea."

I was about to tell him he was making a TERRIBLE decision, but *wait*... I stopped myself just in time.

Ash *didn't* need to do magic to be extraordinary. What was it Ms Sparks had said? *There are more ways to get to the moon than on a broom!*

6:47pm Home

Ash came home with me to meet Egg *properly*. He's not even a little bit cross with me now and I cheered him up even more by telling him about all the friendly *mingling* in the tea tent, but there's still something bothering me. Not the fact that Egg's shell has gone all spider-webby with cracks; not the fact that she's glowing even more than yesterday; not even the fact that she is really very warm indeed! It's not even that I'm meant to be handing her over to Professor Agu tonight (although that is making me feel quite *gulpy*). It's the *bonfire party*. Everyone says it's the time for friends to come *together*, but even though Ash and I have cleared the air, and even though he's *cool* with me doing magic, he can't come and that seems so unfair. In fact, it SUCKS.

"It won't be the same without you there," I say to him over and over, making both our tummies rumble with tales of the Winter Solstice Log. I was just going to get my mask to show him when I heard the yelling outside.

"Bea!"

"Beeeeeeeeaaaa!"

"BBBBBEEEEAAAA!"

Fat snowballs started smacking against the front window.

"You go," said Ash, getting up. "I'll let myself out the back door."

"NO!" I said so firmly he sat down again in surprise. "Don't go anywhere."

Maybe Ash couldn't come to the Extraordinary bonfire party, but it was time for him to meet my Extraordinary friends.

And before I could change my mind, I flung open the door to see ... *a phoenix, a bat, a griffin and a hippogriff standing on the doorstep!* The masks were even more realistic now they were on.

"We came to see if you were OK," said the phoenix (Winnie). "You left school in such a hurry."

"I'm *fine*," I said (because now I was). "And I'm glad you came round because my friend Ash is here and I want you all to meet him. *Properly*."

They looked at each other in panic and whipped off their masks. A minute later, everyone was standing in the kitchen, introducing themselves. All my friends together just like I'd wanted and it was...

REALLY AWKWARD!

Eeeeugh! They were all being so *polite*. This wasn't what I'd imagined! I didn't just want my Extraordinary friends and Ash to say 'hello' like aliens from different planets. I wanted them to know him like *I* knew him. And I wanted *him* to know *them* like I knew them and that was never going to happen if they were trying to hide their magic from him. If we were going to hang out together like real friends, *it was time*.

I gulped, put my hands on Egg's warm, glowing shell for courage and blurted it out. "*HE KNOWS*."

"He knows what?" asked Amara.

"I know that you're all w-witches," Ash said bravely.

For a minute they all looked at each other in panic.

"OK," said Puck at last. "So he knows. The question is, what are we going to do about it?"

"Memory-wiping spell of course," Fabi said briskly and everyone looked at Winnie.

"Sorry," she said. "That's a Year Ten spell." She hesitated. "I suppose I could have a go ... but I might wipe his memory completely forever. Or I might accidentally SHRINK him – the spells are quite similar."

"Er ... I would not be OK with that," said Ash faintly.

Fabi gave him a long stare. "You're not going to tell anyone, are you?"

"No," said Ash. "I'm not."

"*Sure?*" Amara looked worried.

"*Pfffff*, it's not like anyone would believ—" Ash began, saw us all glaring at him, changed his mind and said solemnly, "I *promise*." He held up his hand like he was making an oath.

"And none of *you* are going to tell anyone that he knows?" I asked the others and then somehow we were all holding hands and pledging to keep the secret safe. And it's true what people say about a secret shared being a secret halved* because I felt better immediately.

"So you can stop worrying, Bea," said Ash, "and go to your party."

"I still wish you could come," I said for the hundredth time.

"Me too!" he said and the others, who had decided very quickly that Ash was a good egg, all nodded.

And that was when Puck had his BRAINWAVE.** "Maybe he *can*..." He grinned. "This isn't just any old bonfire party ... it's a Winter Solstice Extraordinary *MASKED* bonfire party! All we need to do is make Ash a mask and then he can come with us. Simple!"

OK, it wasn't *that* simple. We didn't have enchanted paint for a start, but there was a lot of card and glue left over from Dad's banner-making and Winnie spelled the ordinary paint I found so

*Sixth'd??
**If it works...

that at least it was the right colour, and twenty minutes later, a surprisingly passable WOLF mask was lying on the kitchen table.

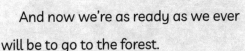

"I'll just spell your hair the right colour," said Puck and, before Ash could stop him, it was done.

And now we're as ready as we ever will be to go to the forest.

ALL of us!!!

8:00pm The Secret Glade, the forest

I might be in the middle of the wildest, funnest, fieriest, most Winter Solstice-y party of my life with all my friends, but I had to find a quiet tree-trunk hollow and take a minute to write this down because ... *EGG's hatched!!!!!*

Wait, I'm going to go back a bit because a lot has happened...

The party was in full swing by the time we got there, the flames from the huge bonfire leaping up to the stars and sending showers of tiny, fiery sparkles into the frosty air. Pupil-witches in creature masks and teacher-witches, not in masks but in the tallest, pointiest hats I'd ever seen, were leaping and dancing, chanting verses of the *Ode*. It was WILD!

"Hurry!" shouted someone. "Sir Scary Cook's about to cut the Winter Solstice Chocolate Log!"

"Get a slice for me," I called, watching as the others raced – Ash in tow – towards the massive table under a tree, lit up by the golden glow of the fire. I couldn't risk Egg in the crush!

Minutes later, they were back.

"This is AAAMMMAAAAAZZINGGGG!" said Ash, not even noticing the tiny flames leaping out of his mouth as he chewed. "It tastes *more* of chocolate than any chocolate I've ever eaten before!"

I took a big bite. He was right! And then we were all munching and Ash nearly fell over when he noticed the flames coming out of *our* mouths, and we laughed at him, but in a nice way. Even if his mask wasn't *exactly* the same as all the others and *even if* he was never going to try any magic again, he fitted right in with my friends. I took another bite of Winter Solstice Chocolate Log and *wait* ... OF COURSE he fits in! I should have known because that had been my Witchy Wish!

"Excellent frog mask," said a familiar voice. *Eeeeek!* I'm going to take a wild guess ... Bea Black? The *extra* frog on your head and that egg in your arms does rather give it away!"

It was Ms Sparks. She smiled at the others, did a double take and said, "Ah! I see you've brought a friend. You must introduce me."

Broomsticks! Just when everything was going so well. "He's um … Puck's c-cousin," I stammered. "A very *w-witchy* cousin … from er T-Transylvania."

Ms Sparks raised an eyebrow. "That's a long way to come."

"Oh, he flew here in no time. LOVES parties!" Puck was trying to help.

"Well … welcome, Mr…?"

"B-Boris," I said quickly. "Mr Boris."

"Oh, Bea!"

Was Ms Sparks trying not to laugh? It wasn't *that* funny a name.

"Just so you know –" she leaned in and whispered in my ear – "*it's been illegal to turn anyone into a toad since 1532.*"

But before I could work out what she meant by *that*, another teacher had joined us.

"Professor Agu!" Ms Sparks welcomed him with a sweep of her magnificent pointy witch hat. "Is it time?"

The professor beamed and nodded. Then, with a single flick of his wand, he conjured up the most

beautiful soft nest on the ground
and gestured to me to put Egg down.

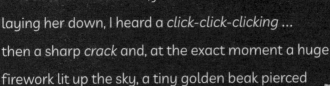

It *WAS* time because, just as I was
laying her down, I heard a *click-click-clicking* ...
then a sharp *crack* and, at the exact moment a huge
firework lit up the sky, a tiny golden beak pierced
Egg's shell!

Oh!

Seconds later, the strangest little creature I'd ever
seen was blinking in the glow of the flames and
shaking off shards of shell.

"Is it a bird?" suggested Amara doubtfully.

"Birds aren't *furry*." Izzi rolled her eyes. Everyone
was coming over for a look.

The creature yawned and shook out little, leathery
wings. "Oooooh, it's a bat!" said Puck.

"Bats don't come out of eggs, **toadbrain**," said
Blair. "And they're not PINK."

"Well, it's not a baby dragon," said a dragon-mask-
wearing witch.

Whatever it was, it looked round at us all with

beady little eyes, hopped out of the shell, lurched unsteadily up into the air and settled on my left shoulder!

"Well done, little one!" I said, stroking its pink furry tummy very gently and ignoring Stan who was glaring at it suspiciously from my right shoulder.

"BUT WHAT IS IT?" persisted about twenty witches all at once.

"It's a Finkelspark," said Professor Agu. "Of course!"

"*Ooooooooh*," we chorused. "*Of course!*" (Although, judging by the confused looks, I don't think I was the only witch never to have heard of a Finkelspark before.)

"Terribly rare," said the professor. "Legend has it that they only hatch once every one hundred and one years." He came closer and muttered something to Egg – she'll always be Egg to me – in a language I didn't understand. "But now it's time for her to go."

I felt a little teary. "Will I ever see her again?"

"If you *need* to," said the professor and then he patted me on the arm. "You did a good job, Bea. Well done."

For a few seconds, Egg hovered in front of me, her little wings stirring the sparky air, and then with a **WHOOSH** she shot up into the night sky...

Up, up, up she went, a little pink speck turning darker as it got further and further away until I couldn't see her any more.

But I won't forget her EVER and that's why I'm writing all this down.

"*Come on, Bea!*"

"*Hurry up, BEAAA!*"

My friends are yelling for me.

"*Put that diary away!*"

I'm running out of pages anyway...

"*Come on!*" They're all shouting.

"*Time to PAARRTY!!!*"

Things I Will ACHIEVE
Next Term!

- Get better at the Flying Cat Swerve and the Boggle Dodge and try to master the Skeleshaker and – if brave enough – the STEALTHY SLITHER.

- Persuade Dad to buy me a puppy ... but even more importantly persuade Mr Muddy and rest of class to let me stay on frog rota FOREVER because I ♥ STAN.

- Be the best vice-captain of the Dodos since the time of Minerva Moon.

- Find out who Minerva Moon is was!

- Get better at cooking/potions/baking.

- Ask Blair to teach me how to do the loop-the-loop on my broom WITHOUT FALLING OFF.

- Hang out with all my friends TOGETHER!